MW01075082

**THIS
GIRL
FOR
HIRE**

THIS
GIRL
FOR
HIRE

G. G. Fickling

THE OVERLOOK PRESS
Woodstock • New York

This edition first published in paperback in the United States in 2005 by
The Overlook Press, Peter Mayer Publishers, Inc.
New York & Woodstock

NEW YORK:
141 Wooster Street
New York, NY 10012

WOODSTOCK:
One Overlook Drive
Woodstock, NY 12498
www.overlookpress.com
[for individual orders, bulk and special sales, contact our Woodstock office]

Copyright © 1956 by Gloria and Forrest E. Fickling

All Rights Reserved. No part of this publication may be reproduced or
transmitted in any form or by any means, electronic or mechanical, including
photocopy, recording, or any information storage and retrieval system now
known or to be invented without permission in writing from the publisher,
except by a reviewer who wishes to quote brief passages in connection with
a review written for inclusion in a magazine, newspaper, or broadcast.

Originally published in 1957 by Pyramid Books

Library of Congress Cataloging-in-Publication Data

Fickling, G. G., 1925-
This girl for hire / G.G. Fickling.—1st ed.
p. cm.
1. Women private investigators—California—Los Angeles—Fiction.
2. Los Angeles (Calilf.)—Fiction. I. Title: Honey West. II. Title.
PS3556.I327T48 2005   813'.6—dc22.....2005049848

Book design and type formatting by Bernard Schleifer
Manufactured in Canada
FIRST EDITION
ISBN 1-58567-684-5
1 3 5 7 9 8 6 4 2

To Tina and Richard Prather.
Ongalabongay! And to Shell Scott
who can play house with Honey
any old time!

THIS
GIRL
FOR
HIRE

ONE

WIND DROVE IN UNDER THE EVES, SPATTERING DROPS of night rain on the dead man's mutilated face.

Lieutenant Mark Storm got to his feet, lit a cigarette and studied the battered corpse. Then he glanced at me.

"You want a cigarette?"

"No, thanks," I said softly. "I haven't got the stomach for one right now. When'll the coroner be here?"

Mark walked to the shade-drawn window and peeked out at the storm. Then he said, "Few minutes, I guess. Honey, gal, you'd better go home. It's late."

"Come on, Lieutenant," I said. "You don't have to play games with me. I've seen blood before."

He whirled around. "I told you to get out of here. Now get out! That's an order."

"Herb Nelson was a client of mine. I've got a right to be here."

Mark took off his hat and nervously dented his

knuckles in the crown. "Look, I don't care whether you're a private detective or not. This guy looks as if he's been hit by a freight train. No self-respecting woman would stay in the same room with such a torn-up mess, much less ogle at it"

Music drifted out of the distant night. An odd sound, distorted by the wind in the trees. It was a sad song with a high-pitched trumpet that reminded me of taps being played over a dreary, cold burial ground. It seemed a sorry end for a man who had fought his way to the very top of the entertainment world and then toppled to the very bottom.

"I'll take that cigarette now," I said.

Mark slammed his hat back on his head. He started to form a new argument with his mouth and then gave it up, handing me a cigarette. "You kill me, Honey. A gal with your class, looks, personality—" He shook his head dismally. "What in hell did he hire you for?"

"To find out who was trying to kill him."

Mark Storm, a cynic from the day he was born, lit my cigarette, blew the match out with an expression of disgust and said, "All right, who killed him? A Santa Fe streamliner?"

"I wouldn't be surprised. Know any likely ones with a record?"

"You kill me—" he started.

"You said that."

He turned on his heels and crossed the small, dingy second-story room to a shelf crammed with odds and ends. Under a pile of dirty laundry he extracted an

Academy Award Oscar. Also a .38 revolver. He flipped open the cylinder and peered at me through the six empty chambers. "Did he have a permit for this thing?"

"I don't know. Ask him."

"Don't be funny," Mark said, tossing the gun back on the shelf. "When we go out for an evening and you stop off to check on a client who's been hit by an H-bomb, I want straight talk, do you understand?"

The music kept sadly drifting in. In a way this was funny. Not laughable, but the sad kind of funny that makes you say things you don't mean. Mark didn't sound like Lieutenant Mark Storm of the sheriff's office, homicide. He sounded like a little boy who suddenly felt the first pangs of manhood when he told his little sister to go home after they found the dead remains of their dog. And I sounded like the sister, who, fighting back desperate tears, made light of his brave attempts to protect me.

With Mark standing firm-legged and angry in the middle of Herb Nelson's dismal, one-room apartment, I said, "I liked the guy. He was a terrific person. He didn't have any money. He didn't have any close friends. But he had a mountain full of guts. Now stop acting the part of a deputy sheriff. I know you liked him, too. Everybody did."

Mark creased his hat again. "This is murder!" he said with a little boy's anger.

"How do you know it's murder?" I demanded. "Maybe he *was* hit by a train. Maybe he threw himself in front of it. Maybe someone who knew him picked him up and brought his body back here."

"You know better than that!"

I did know better than that, but I didn't want to admit it. You couldn't accept this as murder when you knew what Herb Nelson had been to a generation of children who'd grown up in the thirties and forties. He had been as widely celebrated as F.D.R., Hopalong Cassidy or the Wizard of Oz. I could still remember the songs they had written about him, the jokes that were told, the great performances he'd given on the motion-picture screens. I suddenly felt that wave of female nausea Mark had expected me to feel earlier.

"I want to get out of here," I said unhappily.

Mark's legs loosened from their angry stance. He replaced his hat and crossed to me.

"I—I'm sorry, Honey," he said. "Believe me, I'm sorry."

"So am I, Mark. And I'm mad, too, at the very same time. I'm mad because—because—nobody had the right to do this. I don't care what he did after—he wasn't big any more. Do you know what I mean?"

"Yeah," he said softly, putting an arm around my shoulder. "Yeah, I know what you mean." He swallowed and it was a deep swallow of hate for something seemingly untouchable, but with a hope that it could be touched some day, somehow. "Some dirty bastard!" he said.

The coroner and several men from the sheriff's office arrived a few minutes later. They were all young men in their thirties and they couldn't believe their eyes. It seemed utterly impossible, but there it was. A child's dream all smashed to pieces. The coroner guessed Herb had been dead about four hours.

After they took his body away to the morgue, Mark and I drove south to a little coffee house in Laguna. The rain still pelted down and the surf crashed awesomely in tune with the storm's fury.

I stirred a spoonful of sugar into my coffee and watched the crystals melt away in the black depths. Then I said, "Herb never paid me a cent. I want you to know that. He tried to, but I wouldn't take it."

Mark stared through the open door at the rain drops shimmering in the brilliance of the neon sign. "Who was he afraid of, Honey? Was he really worried somebody was going to kill him?" He squeezed his big knuckles with the weight of his other hand. "Who the hell did he suspect?"

I sipped my coffee, listening to the faint roar of an airliner battling through the stormy sky. "You don't understand, Mark."

Headlights of oncoming traffic on Pacific Coast Highway flickered across the big lieutenant's eyes making them glitter weirdly like cat's eyes caught in the same reflection. "Listen, Miss Private Eye!" he barked. "A man's dead. I've got to explore every possible lead. Now give!"

I shook my head. "All right. About a month ago, Herb landed a bit part in a Bob Swanson TV show. He got into some kind of hassle with the star and cast. There were some pretty bitter words. Herb was apparently hitting the bottle and I guess he went berserk when

Swanson ordered him off the set. He started swinging and before it was all over an expensive camera was damaged and a set wrecked at Television Riviera.

Mark scowled. "That doesn't spell murder in my book. Come on, Honey, you're holding out on me. What is it?"

"Well, as I understand it, Swanson threatened Herb during the fracas. Then, a week later, Herb got a letter signed by Swanson, followed by several phone calls."

"Where's the letter?"

"Herb said he was so mad he tore it up and burned the scraps. He said the letter contained insulting remarks about his acting. Even suggested Herb would be better off dead."

"That still doesn't add up to murder," Mark said, pushing his cup away. "What about the phone calls?"

"More threats. Herb said it was the same voice each time. It could have been Swanson, but he wasn't absolutely certain. Something was used to muffle the voice. Probably a handkerchief."

"Have you checked out Swanson?" Mark demanded. "To a certain extent. He's a baby-faced, muscular schizophrenic actor with a yearly paycheck of at least a million. As far as I could find out, he had no reason in the world to threaten Herb Nelson—aside from his fight on the sound stage at WBS-TV."

"Who else was on the set at the time of the blowup?"

"Cameramen, grips, electricians—the usual TV backstage crew," I said. "The producer on the Swanson show is a guy named Sam Aces. Joe Meeler writes the series and Swanson does his own directing. They were all present when the fireworks started. So were about six actors and actresses."

Mark wiped some of the dampness off his forehead and squinted up at the wall menu. "What do you think of the Swanson theory?"

"'The whole business sounds too pat. That's why I didn't kick the information over to your office. What do you think?"

"Yeah," he grunted. "Nobody in his right mind sends a letter telling a person he'd 'be better off dead, signs his own John Henry and then drives up with a tank loaded with a twenty-millimeter cannon."

"I went all the way back to the day Herb was born. He never had an enemy in the world. When he worked at Metro, he was the most liked person in the studio—barring none."

Mark, a man who had lived, breathed and formulated his ideals during the era of Herb Nelson, drew an exasperated breath. "Why not? How—how anybody could kill a man of Herb Nelson's stature—and like that—" He drifted off into a niche of chronic hatred all policemen have for a murder which jolts them into the realization that despite the badge and the training, they are still human beings and subject to remorse for the victim and loathing for the wrongdoer.

"He grew up in Pasadena," I said. "An orphan. No record of who his parents were, where he was born, nothing. Not a birth certificate anywhere. Herb started acting when he was in his teens. He was the kind of guy who ended up class president, most likely to succeed, most popular—"

"All right," Mark said angrily. "Where do we stand? Somebody must have hated his guts. Who was it?"

"How do I know?"

"He hired you to protect his life, didn't he?"

I knew what was coming. It was the same old thing. Mark didn't like private eyes. Especially the female variety. He was always frying to prove the superhuman portraits of them in fiction were the most dismal fraud ever perpetrated.

He turned and stared at me with about as much compassion as a little boy would feel staring at the spoon after he'd swallowed the castor oil. "Why didn't he come to me about these threats? We might have prevented this!"

"Sure," I said sarcastically. "You probably get at least a dozen calls a week from people who say their lives are in danger. Do you save every one?"

"No!" Mark roared. "But we would have saved Herb Nelson!"

"Yeah, I'll bet!" I got to my feet "It's late. I want to go back to my office."

"Sure," he said, tossing some change on the counter. "You might have a customer—with real dough, and an option on a plot at Forest Lawn cemetery."

Anger was forming a big knot in my throat, but I managed to answer, "Why don't you get a new subject, Lieutenant? You've worn this one down to the nub."

We walked out into the rain. It touched my face, recalling days long ago when I waited in the same kind of downpour, blonde curls clinging to my forehead, and hoped my father, a private detective, would come out of the wet darkness, still safe and sound and smiling.

When we reached Long Beach, the rain stopped and the wheels of Mark's car whined dismally on the slick pavement. I listened to the sound for a long time and then said, "Sure, I feel bad about Herb Nelson. I feel partially responsible that he's dead. Wouldn't anybody under the same circumstances?"

Mark kept his eyes on the windshield-wiped panorama of street lights that faintly illuminated Anaheim Street in Long Beach. "Honey, why don't you get out of this business? What are you trying to prove?"

"What do you think?"

"So your father was murdered! That's no reason to keep banging your head against the wall!"

I jerked around in the seat as if I felt the same bullet which had ended Hank West's career in a dirty Los Angeles back alley. "You've got a lot of guts to tell me what I ought to do—where I ought to get off! Sure, I'm a woman! I act like a woman, think like a woman, look like a woman, but I'm mixed up in a rotten dirty business that men think they own by right of conquest! But you've never stopped to consider that half the crimes in the United States today are committed by women—and half of those committed by men are provoked by women. So where does that leave you? In a business operated seventy-five percent by females! All right, so you don't think I'm nice. What are you going to do about it?"

Mark looked at me with the contemptible expression of a man who hates himself because he doesn't understand why he likes something he thinks he should hate. "The only thing nice about you," he said hotly, "are your legs. You should have been a chorus girl."

The left-handed compliment bounced off me like buckshot off a fleeing watermelon thief. It went just far enough in to hurt. "Thanks," I murmured. "If the opportunity ever arises, I'll take advantage of it."

"I'm sure you will," Mark said, spinning the wheels and pulling to the curb outside my office.

I opened the door and stepped out, a jolting angry step that rang on the cement. Mark followed me up the stairway to the third floor. At the end of the hall was a glass door with the words, H. WEST, PRIVATE INVESTIGATOR painted in gold-leaf serif letters.

Mark gestured at the door. "You see, you don't even have the guts to let 'em know you're a woman before they walk in."

"I'm not in this business for my health," I said, inserting my key into the lock.

"What are you in it for?" Mark demanded hotly.

I didn't bother to answer. I was in this business for a lot of reasons, many of which he knew but refused to accept. I was tired of being accused, insulted and pushed around for doing a job men considered wrong for a woman.

The office was cold and damp. A brassiere hung out of an open desk drawer where I'd left it during a quick change earlier in the day.

Mark casually walked over and lifted the article of clothing up. "What kind of business did you say you were running?"

I slammed the door. "You want to know something, Lieutenant?" I said. "I'm going to find the person who murdered Herb Nelson, and when I do I'm going to take that piece of underwear and wrap it around your big thick neck!"

Mark threw down the bra and a grin spread across face. "That's a deal!" he said.

TWO

HERB NELSON'S BRUTAL MURDER MADE BIG HEADLINES the next morning. The Los Angeles press called it, "The worst crime since the Black Dahlia!"

One of the major newspapers handled the story pictorially with two pages of photos, including one gruesome posed shot of Herb Nelson's blood-stained hand clutching his Academy Award Oscar.

Rain continued to pour from the stormy sky, filling the gutters. After breakfast I called Fred Sims, an old friend of mine who was a reporter on the *Long Beach Press-Telegram*. Fred walked with a cane, but still managed to cover every inch of mayhem committed in Southern California. He said he was going to have breakfast at a hamburger joint on the Pike and asked me to join him for a cup of coffee.

We sat under a badly worn awning while Fred munched on a sandwich. Finally, he muttered, "Herb Nelson was a client of yours?"

"Yeah."

"You got an exclusive story for me?"

"Nope."

Fred pulled his lean, slightly bent frame around in his seat. He had deep, steel-gray eyes that ate through a person like acid through a piece of tin. "Well, what do you want?"

I created a few half-gestures that were reminiscent of a tired seagull about to set down on the water for a rest. "I hate to admit it, but I need some advice, Fred."

He grinned, lifted up his cane and took a practiced sight, one eye narrowed on the careening, empty roller-coaster cars in the distance.

"How old are you, Honey?" he asked.

"Twenty-eight. Now come on, Fred, let's not kid around—"

"You want my advice?"

"Well sure, but—"

The crippled newspaperman lowered his cane and rapped it on the cement "Look, I don't have time to kid with you or anyone else. Now do you want my advice or not?"

He sounded like a soldier I'd read about during the war who refused to quit in the face of tremendous odds and led an infantry assault with his leg practically blown off. The soldier's name had been Fred Sims, and he hadn't changed a bit. He still refused to listen to any one or wait for an answer. "Go to Hollywood," he said.

"What?"

"Close up your office for a couple of weeks. Go to Hollywood and get a job."

"What for?" I demanded.

Fred chewed on some soggy potato chips, then shoved the plate away. "You want to find Nelson's murderer, don't you?"

"Of course—"

"What do you measure, Honey?"

"What?"

"What do you measure?"

"Where?"

He smiled, got up and with the aid of his cane, circled my chair. "Everywhere," he said pointedly.

"What's that got to do—"

"Answer my question!" he barked stubbornly.

I groaned. "38-22-36. Five feet five. One hundred and twenty pounds. Normal childhood diseases. No dimples. Small birthmark on inside of right thigh. Parents both dead. No known living relatives." I stood up and snapped him a salute. "Anything else, General?"

"Yeah, can you act?"

"Of course not I've never been on a stage in my life."

"That doesn't matter. With your taffy-colored hair, blue eyes and baby-bottom complexion, you ought to set Hollywood on fire with your looks alone."

"Thanks, pal," I said, "but who would hire me? There must be a thousand real-live dolls living in Hollywood and starving. It's a great idea. Sure, if I could get into the studios through the actor's entrance instead of through the private eye's keyhole, I'd probably land something fast. But without experience I wouldn't get past the casting desk."

Fred wiped his eyes with the back of his hand. "Yeah, 'I guess you're right. Well, it was a good idea while it lasted. Would have made a great story. Terrific headline. Succulent Shamus Shucks Stiletto for Stardom."

"Very funny."

We started back toward town, Fred's metal-tipped cane cracking hollowly on the cement. Thoughts about Herb Nelson's blowup at Television Riviera drummed the same rhythmic cadence in my head. Was the killer affiliated with Bob Swanson's TV show? Was he the director, the producer, the cameraman?"

Sunlight broke through brightening the dull sky as Fred turned off down Ocean Avenue. He grinned, threw me a kiss and vanished in the mid-day crowd.

I continued on to my building, climbed the two flights of stairs and tried the doorknob. It wouldn't budge. The office door was never locked during the day, but apparently I'd been careless this time and snapped the latch on my way out to see Fred.

I rummaged futilely in my bag for the key. Then, recalling that one of my office windows opened onto the fire escape, I went downstairs, around to the alley and climbed up the metal staircase to the third floor.

The window was open just wide enough for me to squeeze through on my stomach.

When I got inside and turned around, the cold ugly snout of a gun was pressed squarely between my eyes.

Looking up the barrel of a loaded revolver is an experience not many people have the opportunity to put into words. For a long instant I was speechless.

Then I managed to say something which didn't make any sense at all, except that it was the truth. "I—haven't paid my insurance premium this month."

"What do you want?" a male voice snapped.

"I might ask you the same question. This is my office."

"Your—" the voice stopped. What are you talking about? This is H. West's office. He's a private detective."

"He was," I said, "until somebody did what you look as if you're planning to do."

"You mean there is no H. West? He's dead?"

"That's right," I said. "I'm his daughter. The name's Honey. I'm running the business now."

The revolver lifted up, and the hand that was holding it tossed the weapon on my desk. I focused in on a short dark mustache, a large hooked nose and a pair of black horn-rimmed glasses. "I—I'm sorry," he said. "I didn't know. I thought you were somebody else."

"Who were you expecting?" I asked, trying to shake off the tingle in my spine.

"Bob Swanson. He's trying to kill me."

"Bob Swanson? The TV actor?"

The man with the mustache had curly black hair and he ran his fingers through it nervously. "Yeah, the very same. My name's Aces—Sam Aces. I produce his show."

"What are you doing here?"

"I—I need help. No kidding. Somebody followed me from L.A. Even came into this building. That's why I locked the door. I figured when H. West came back he'd use a key. Then you appeared at the window and

I got all shook up, grabbed the gun and—"

"Why do you think Swanson wants to kill you?"

Aces nervously lit two cigarettes and handed me one of them. "He'd like to get me out and produce the show himself."

"There must be an easier way!" I said suspiciously.

"I own the rights to the show. Besides, I got a long-term contract with WBS-TV. He couldn't budge me any other way. He's tried to poison me twice."

I drew a mental picture of the TV star, Bob Swanson. He was the athletic type with a round boyish face and muscular arms. "I've watched him on television," I said. "He doesn't strike me as the poison type. A golf club in a dark alley, maybe. He could always say he was having a couple of practice shots and didn't see you."

Aces blew a few smoke rings. Then he said, "Two weeks ago I was working late in Studio Sixteen. I thought everyone had gone home hours before. Suddenly old B.S. came staggering in out of nowhere with a couple of drinks in his chubby little fists. He said he'd been around the corner at a bar called the Golden Slipper lapping up a few when he thought about poor old Sammy back at the studio. He handed me a drink. It was a screw-driver. That's all I ever drink. Anything with orange juice. So I faked a healthy swallow and sent him on his merry way. The next morning I had the contents of that glass analized. It was loaded with four grains of white arsenic."

"Did this report reach the police?" I demanded.

"Yes," Aces said quickly. "Naturally I didn't cooperate

when I learned Max Decker, the owner of WBS-TV, had been with Swanson when that drink was ordered."

"You don't think Decker—?"

"I don't know," Aces said, stubbing out his cigarette. "Max has never been fond of me. So you can see what would have happened if I'd spilled my story to the police. They'd have brought Decker in, too. Max wouldn't like that sort of thing. If I couldn't have proved absolutely it was Swanson who loaded that drink—long-time contract or not—Decker and B.S. would have killed me in the TV field."

"You would have been killed, period, if you'd downed that screwdriver," I said.

"Yeah, I know, and that's what brings me here. Last night we did a live Swanson show themed around a bathing-beauty contest. The winner was supposed to be signed to a six-week contract. But we couldn't get together on the choice. Before the show we held the judging in Decker's office. Max liked one, B.S. liked another and me, well, hell, I didn't really care just so we got the show on the road. I got pretty nervous so I went downstairs to a little juice bar on the first floor. I ordered my usual when B.S. suddenly appeared. We got into an argument about the judging and I guess I wasn't watching him too closely. Next thing I knew he'd gone back up to the studio, leaving me with the ultimatum that if I didn't bring a winner up in five minutes he'd personally knock my brains out. So I gulped down the orange juice and rushed upstairs. I folded up right in the middle of Decker's office."

I said, "You figure Swanson slipped something in your drink during the argument?"

"That's what I don't know. Ann Claypool, one of the bathing-beauty contestants, grabbed a glass of milk and forced some down my throat. I was sick as a dog for a few minutes, then I felt fine."

"Did you feel stomach pains after drinking the orange juice?"

"I felt something," Aces said, "but I don't know whether it was really pain or just in my mind."

"But the milk," I said. "It caused a reaction."

"I'm allergic to milk. It makes me deathly ill."

"Did you know Herb Nelson?" I asked.

"Sure," he said, growing solemn. "I was a good friend to Herb Nelson. We worked together years ago when I was producing at Metro. In fact, I was the guy who dug up the script that won him an Academy Award."

"What caused the argument last month when Herb tore up the studio at Television Riviera?"

Aces didn't hesitate. "Swanson, as usual. I hired Herb for a bit part—an old broken-down comedian. He needed work bad and was drinking pretty heavy. Well, old B.S. bitched when he saw what a tremendous actor Herb was. He criticized Herb, changed his part, made a fool out of him. Herb finally blew his top. He told old B.S. off and then started wrecking the set. We had to call the cops."

"How did Swanson feel after they took Nelson away?"

"Mad as a hornet. Herb hit Swanson with a flood lamp and really floored him."

"Who do you think killed Nelson?"

Aces said, "Who do you think I think? Herb was a nice guy. Only a maniac would do something like that."

"Have you ever had any maniacal moments, Mr. Aces?"

"What are you getting at?"

"You were present when the fireworks started. Are you sure Herb Nelson didn't say anything derogatory about you?"

"Of course not!" His deep eyes rolled angrily. "Say, what is this? I came here to hire someone to help me, not to be accused of harming one of my oldest friends."

Sam Aces appeared to be about fifty. He was tall and gangly with an ambling body that seemed plucked out of some animated cartoon about comical dizzy-eyed giraffes. Despite his poor features, he had a look of warmth and sincerity. He was the kind of person you somehow wanted to like.

"You're perfect," he said after a moment "B.S. is crazy about beautiful dames—especially blondes. Will you work for me?"

"That all depends on what kind of work you want done," I said.

"This afternoon I want you to go see Swanson at Television Riviera. We still haven't picked a winner in our beauty contest. Ten to one he'll go for you. All I have to do is second the motion and you'll be in. You've got to be around when we go on location. He's going to get me, I know he is—unless—"

"But, wait a minute, Mr. Aces—"

"Call me Sam, baby."

"Look, Sam," I protested, "this six-week contract—you know I'm not an actress."

"Who cares? With your face and figure—"

"But I can't learn lines—"

"Lines?" Aces said. "Who learns lines in television? This is the modern age, Honey. We've got little men who do nothing all day but type scripts into big letters on machines. Acting's a cinch. Ask Swanson. He spends two days on the golf course, two days drunk and two days in bed. On the seventh day, he condescends to stand in front of a camera, read from the carding device and look at women with shapely navels." He shrugged his lanky frame. "What do you say? If I go to the police, the publicity will kill me dead. You're the only one who can really help me now. I don't want to windup like Herb Nelson in an adjoining grave."

I scanned his face for a hint of phony melodramatics, but it revealed nothing but despair. His jaw sagged slightly.

"All right," I said. "I'll see what I can do."

We shook hands. Mentally, I considered the possibility of Sam Aces having killed Herb Nelson, then quickly discarded the idea. He seemed honestly afraid. It was the same kind of fear I'd seen in Herb Nelson's eyes the week before his death. As Aces filled out information forms, I kept wanting to tell him I couldn't guarantee his staying out of a six-foot hole. But I never got the words out, because that's exactly where I pictured him. I don't know why, except at that moment Sam Aces' slouched, dejected shoulders and unhappy drawn face gave him the look of a man who was about to die.

THREE

AT FOUR O'CLOCK THAT AFTERNOON I STOOD IN THE center of one of Television Riviera's mammoth sound stages wearing a skin-tight bathing suit. Max Decker, a ponderous bear of a man, sat on two wooden chairs, chewing on a black cigar and squinting under thick brows at my torso. Bob Swanson stood a few feet away, flexing his muscles and undressing me with his eyes.

Sam Aces was in a glass-faced monitor booth above the stage floor. His voice suddenly boomed out over a speaker, "Well, what do you think of her?"

Decker grunted, got a new grip on his cigar and continued to peer at me. Bob Swanson glanced at the booth. "You may be a lousy producer, Sam, but you can sure pick the girls. I vote yes. Can she act?"

"Of course," Aces lied.

"Okay," Swanson said. "What do you say, Max?"

Apparently Decker liked looking at females wearing bathing suits, but couldn't cope with the emotional problem that went with it. "Damn you, Sam!" he barked. "You had to go think up this crazy contest idea, then you went and filled up my office with a lot of fat female fannies, now you come up with a dame who's got more dangerous curves than Indianapolis Speedway and who makes me feel like an H-Bomb about to be triggered. Get her out of here!"

"But, Max!" Swanson protested. "I want this girl."

"Well, have her!" Decker blared back. "Just get her out of my sight. And keep her out of bathing suits!"

I changed my clothes, signed a six-week contract at four hundred a week, then left with Sam Aces.

"What's wrong with Decker?" I asked.

Aces grinned. "High blood pressure. I don't blame him for getting mad. You must have raised his reading at least twenty degrees."

"What about Swanson? I thought he was going to hang around for the contract-signing business?"

"Honey," Aces said patiently, "there's one thing you'll learn about Swanson. The minute the sun goes down he heads for the nearest bar."

"And where would that be?"

"Just around the corner. You know, the place I told you about. The Golden Slipper."

I said good night to Sam, warned him to stay away from orange juice and then walked to the Golden Slipper. It was a ritzy little place with an ornate front and a bar that was as dark as the bottom of the River Styx. I signalled the bartender and ordered a martini. Two seconds later I was joined by the Golden Boy himself, flexing and snorting.

"Hello, baby," Swanson laughed drunkenly. "I hardly recognized you in clothes."

I smiled half-heartedly. "Thanks for the contract, Mr. Swanson."

"Don't thank me. Thank Sam Aces, the miserable bastard. He brought you in."

"You don't like Mr. Aces?"

"That's exactly right, sweetie. In fact, I hate his guts." He took a big gulp of his drink and leaned against the bar for support.

"I don't see how you could feel like that," I said. "He seems like such a nice guy."

Swanson bit hard on his teeth, scowling angrily. "Why that dirty son-of-a—" He stopped, his eyes narrowing suspiciously. "What's it to you?" He banged for another drink. "You make a lot of observations for a blonde walk-on with no talent but plenty of chest muscle. What's your name?"

"Honey West."

"Where'd you get that handle, in burlesque?"

"It's on my birth certificate, Mr. Swanson. No middle name. I was never in burlesque."

He gave me a knowing look. "Baby, you really missed you're calling."

"Now you're making the observations, Mr. Swanson. Why don't you like Sam Aces?"

"You writing a book?"

"Maybe."

Television star, Bob Swanson, winner of last year's award for best male performer, slugged down his fresh drink, wiped off his mouth with the back of his hand and grinned drunkenly. "Okay, put this in your first chapter, baby. You ever hear of an actor named Herb Nelson?"

"Sure—"

"He's dead," Swanson interrupted. "Murdered. You must have read about it in the papers. You want to know who did it? Sam Aces, that's who. And he's going to kill me next. You understand? That is, if I don't get him first!"

"Those are pretty strong words, Mr. Swanson," I said. "Why would Sam Aces want to kill Herb Nelson?"

"I don't know." He answered quickly as if he knew but didn't want to put it into words.

"Second chapter," I said, staring at my martini. "Why do you think he wants to kill you?"

"Power. I got too much power and Aces doesn't like it. There'd be no show without me. Aces can't stand it. He'd like to blow my brains out."

Bob Swanson talked exactly like the frustrated guy he was supposed to be. Prior to Herb Nelson's death I'd spent several hours digging into the muscle man's notoriously unspectacular past. He had migrated to TV from motion pictures after a sporadic career as a temperamental child star and an even more-impossible-to-work-with postwar jungle hero. From that point it had been a series of breaks which had sprung him into the choice situation comedy series about a bachelor-writer who mixed verbs, consonants and beautiful women.

These criss-cross accusations were puzzling. Sam Aces and Golden Boy suspected each other of murdering Herb Nelson and of plotting the same end for each other. I was more inclined to believe my client's story. A phone call earlier to Daws, Inc., a pharmaceutical lab in Beverly Hills, had verified the presence of arsenic in Aces' drink. L.A. police had backed this up with an official report listing the incident as "closed due to insufficient cooperation."

"Third chapter," I said.

"Third chapter," Swanson said, grinning slyly, "is where beautiful blonde with gorgeous blue eyes throws her book out and agrees to accompany handsome young television star on a tour of the night spots. Come on!"

He whisked me into his Cadillac convertible before I could argue. A quick thought struck me. If Bob Swanson had slipped arsenic into Aces' drink, it. was just possible he still might have some of the poison lying around. I wanted to have a look at his personal stationery too. Herb Nelson had said the threat note had been typed on bright orange bond with a giant letter "S" embossed in the corner.

"Why waste time in a bunch of dingy bars?" I leaned against his shoulder. "Why not your place? I bet you even have a swimming pool!"

His eyes lit up like a neon sign. "Have I got a swimming pool?" he roared. "This pool was designed especially for you, baby doll. Wait until you see it!"

We zipped out to Beverly Hills in eleven minutes flat. Bob Swanson's home was fantastically modern. It was so low-slung you had to duck to get through the front door. The house was a gigantic flat-roofed square with a swimming pool in the center. There were no inside walls, only a few moveable partitions, and at each corner of the house there were elevated platforms. These were built much like television sound stages with arc lights in the ceiling and steps leading up. There was only one major difference. They were entirely carpeted with thick foam rubber. From each of them, things happening on any of the other stages could obviously been seen merely by looking over the low-slung, unwalled kitchen, the tremendous indoor swimming pool or the equally unwalled bathrooms. Bob Swanson's home was the most spectacular, and at the same time vulgar looking, place I'd ever seen.

He pointed at the four raised stages. "The bedrooms," he said casually. "This is a four bedroom home."

"But, no beds," I observed. "Where do you sleep?"

"What do you mean, no beds?" Swanson demanded. "Four of the biggest king-size hammocks in captivity. Twelve by twelve. A foot depth of the softest foam rubber you ever snuggled your lily-white rear into, I'll bet!"

"You sleep on the floor?"

Golden Boy grinned. "Natch. Best place to sleep. No falling out of bed. Plenty of room to roam. No pillows. Just pull a blanket over you if it gets a little cold."

I looked at this guy and shook my head. "Did you design the place?"

"Every last inch."

"You don't like privacy, I take it?"

"The hell with privacy," Swanson said. "Notice! No permanent walls. A few partitions for those futile numbskulls who have to hide something that nobody gives a damn about seeing in the first place. You ever think about that? Nothing's worth seeing if it's ugly. The partitions are for the ugly ones. I get a few of those now and then."

He led me to the swimming pool. It was immense and shaped like the body of a very large-bosomed woman.

"What are you, a nudist?" I asked.

Golden Boy raised his eyebrows as if he smelled something foul. "Hell, no. Nobody is ever allowed in this pool in the nude. It contaminates the water. We have bathtubs for that sort of thing. Anyone who swims in this pool wears one of my special suits."

"What?"

"Plastic," he said, pulling one of the suits out of a poolside cabinet "The men wear plastic trunks and the women have plastic pants and bras."

I examined the two-piecer he handed to me. It was fantastic. And transparent. So transparent not even a mole could go undetected underneath. I wondered what kind of queer psychosis affected this man, but undoubtedly it had no conventional name. It was a perfect blend of nature and sanitation. Bob Swanson was what could have been called a natursanicotic. He was crazy about living in the raw, but wanted to keep the microbes caged while he was doing it.

He asked me to go for a swim.

"Let's have a drink first," I suggested quickly. "I'd like to look around the rest of the house."

"Sure, baby." Then he laughed. He was still pretty drunk. "But don't get lost"

My return laugh didn't feel right in my throat. I wondered who'd get the last laugh. If I couldn't find some of that deadly white powder quick, Golden Boy was certain to have me in one of his peek-a-boo bathing suits. There was only one thing on my mind—arsenic. And only one thing on his mind—my chassis. I had to locate what I was after before his plans began to jell.

Swanson switched on his hi-fi and the throbbing rhythm of *Taboo* filled the house. As casually as possible, I mamboed into the modern kitchen area. The all-electric stove, oven, roaster and charcoal broiler were housed in a long, low-slung orange-colored case. The sink faced a floor-to-ceiling window that looked out into a green land-scape. Glancing over at Golden Boy, who was bent over a bar built low enough to serve kids in grammar school, I silently cursed his idea of no walls. You couldn't do a thing around this place unnoticed. I reached quickly down and tried to pull open a cabinet drawer. It wouldn't budge. A try for another drawer yielded the same results. The next instant, he was breathing down my back.

"Wha'cha doing?" he asked curiously.

I turned around slowly. "Oh, nothing. Thought I'd look at your kitchenware. Women go for that sort of thing, you know."

He laughed. I didn't like that laugh. It sounded too much like the last one. "Drawers and cabinets are all electric," he said. "You got to know where to touch them to make 'em work. Cost me a fortune."

"That's a crazy thing. What'd you do that for?"

He led me back to the kindergarten-size bar. "I don't like snoopers," he said. "That's one thing you'll learn about me. I don't trust anyone. I had this setup installed in every moveable object in the joint. It makes me rest easier. This way I know nobody is going through my stuff. Whether I'm here or not."

"But what if somebody learns the spot to touch to open things up?"

He grinned. "Oh, that's easy." He pointed to a tiny metal plate on one of the bar doors. "This is the place to touch, but you got to have this to touch it with. "He held up a piece of metal that was attached to his key chain.

"It's a magnet," he said proudly. "A special magnet. I've got the only one that will spring these locks." He laughed again. "Simple, isn't it?"

I nodded. This was one character who would never be caught with his poison out in the open. In fact, I wouldn't have been surprised if he had a special key and a special vault for such appetizing spices as arsenic.

He handed me an orange-colored drink in a tall glass.

"What's this?" I asked quickly.

"A screwdriver," he said. "If you don't mind my saying so, I make damned good ones."

The drink went crashing to the slate surface that surrounded the swimming pool. Swanson leaped to his feet. I stood, holding an invisible glass, staring blankly at the orange liquid soaking into the stone. It had been a stupid reflex action. Talk about Sam Aces being allergic to milk.

At that moment, I was sure I'd never be able to drink anything with even a hint of orange flavor again.

It took a bit of doing, but I managed to cover over the accident without arousing too much suspicion. He did think it was strange when I turned down a second of his "superb" screwdrivers for an "unspectacular" martini.

Then came swim time.

"What size do you wear?" Golden Boy asked.

"I'm a working girl," I said. "It's getting late. I'd better be getting home."

"You just got here," he said, flexing his biceps. "You have to swim in my pool. That's standard procedure for all female visitors."

"It isn't standard procedure with me."

"You can change right here," he persisted. "I won't mind."

"I'll bet!"

"You're almost twice as broad on top as you are in the middle," he said, scanning my figure.

"I didn't think you noticed," I said sarcastically. "Anyway, you're still not going to get me out of my clothes."

"Get into that bathing suit!" he demanded.

I threw the bra and pants in his face. "You put it on! You designed it, you wear it!"

I should never have done that. His eyes, widened into a passionate glare. He obviously liked women when they got rough.

"I love you!" he yelled. "Nobody's ever done that to me! Nobody!"

He uttered a drunken beastly growl which must have been a throwback to the days when he played a poor man's Tarzan. Then he staggered toward me with his arms outstretched. I thought about using some of the judo tactics I'd learned from my father, but decided in favor of some healthier conversation.

"Now look, Mr. Swanson," I argued. "Let's simmer down, brush back your hair and drive me home."

He kept coming with the determined gait of a full-back driving off tackle. The conversation period was over. I sidestepped, brought my foot up and he went straight into the pool. That was exactly what he needed. A good cooling off. I started for the phone to call a taxi, then thought about Mr. Swanson's swan dive. I glanced at the pool. He hadn't come up!

Bubbles gurgled to the surface where Golden Boy had gone down. Maybe he couldn't swim!

I slipped off my shoes, yanked down the zipper on my dress and dove in.

FOUR

SWANSON WAS FLOATING FACE DOWN A FOOT UNDER water. I slipped the crook of my elbow under his chin and brought him to the surface. A silly thought crossed my mind! Tomorrow's headlines: TV HERO DROWNS IN HIS OWN MICROBES! We reached the edge of the pool and I drifted underneath to get more leverage. I never got it.

His lips suddenly split open, sucked in a tremendous gasp of air and he was after me again. With a roar, Swanson rolled over, locked his legs around my bare middle and we went down, straight to the bottom. This guy was one of the greatest actors I'd ever seen. He'd faked the drowning.

His big hands reached for me. I shook him loose for an instant, got a foot up under his chin and kicked. He buckled slightly. Then I caught him again with my heel, a glancing blow that bounced off his left eyebrow. He recoiled, swallowed some water and finally surfaced. I followed him up.

All the fight was drained out of Mr. TV. He sagged on the stone rim of the pool, glowering at me out of the eye that wasn't swelling up. "Get out of my pool!" he bellowed. "Now I'll have to have it drained and sterilized. I ought to sue you."

I climbed up a ladder on the far side and flashed him a smile that was dripping with dislike. "Why don't you sue me, Mr. Swanson? We could bring the jury down here for a swim—in your plastic suits."

He touched his eye and winced. "I'm cancelling your contract, you can be sure of that! You'll never work for the WBS network. In fact, I'll have you so completely blackballed you won't even be able to get a job in Hell!"

"You ought to have a lot of influence down there," I said.

He groaned, the eye closing into a tight black lump of pain. "Get out of my house! Now! This instant! Get out!"

I slipped on my clothes and called a taxi. In the confused rush of leaving, I left my bag and had to have the cab driver turn around and go back. It was lying on the front steps where Swanson had obviously thrown it. I looked inside. Everything seemed to be in order, except for one important item. My .32 revolver was gone!

The next morning Bob Swanson marched into Studio Sixteen wearing a patch over his left eye. I was going over a TV script with Sam Aces and his chief writer, Joe Meeler. The muscle man stormed toward Aces when he saw me.

"What's this girl doing here?" Swanson bellowed. "I might ask you the same question," Aces said. "Isn't this one of your golf days?"

"No, it is not!"

Aces grinned. "My mistake. The way you look I thought sure someone had used your eye for a hole-in-one."

Swanson's face began to twitch with rage. He demanded my immediate removal from the studio.

"Miss West has a contract," Aces reminded him.

"I don't care! She tried to kill me last night!"

"No fooling?" the lanky producer said, grinning. "What'd she hit you with, the side of a house?"

Swanson turned on Sam Aces. "I warn you Mr. Producer!" he hissed. "If you don't get this girl out of here, I'll—"

"You'll what, B.S.?" Aces taunted. "Kill me? Murder me the way you murdered Herb Nelson?"

Swanson stepped back, a jolting wobbly step of a man who takes a jarring right cross and isn't certain he won't collapse from the blow. "What—what are you talking about?"

"You threatened him, didn't you?" Aces answered quickly. "You told him you wished he were dead. You tried to ruin the poor guy, didn't you?"

"That's ridiculous—"

"You hate everybody, Swanson!" Aces continued viciously. "Anybody who gets up near the top, or guys like Nelson who've hit it and gone down—you shove them good, don't you?"

Swanson whirled angrily and left the studio. I glanced at Sam Aces. A small glint flickered in his deep-set eyes as he stared after the fleeting figure of Bob Swanson. I tried to analyze the look and the incident. Had Sam Aces used the element of surprise to stun an innocent man into seeming guilty? Or was Swanson so obviously the murderer that nothing could help him form a verbal defense against such accusations? Three factors stacked up strongly against Bob Swanson. His name, according to Herb Nelson, had appeared on the threat note. He had accused Aces of murdering Nelson without furnishing any motive for the crime. And it appeared almost certain that he had stolen my .32 revolver.

Privately, I told Aces about the missing gun.

"Great,' the producer groaned. "It wasn't bad enough having to filter all my drinks, now I'll have to filter the air for bullets."

"Swanson must have that gun, Sam. We'd better notify the police."

"No!" Aces said sharply. "We can't do that, Honey. The police'll think I'm crazy. It was bad enough when I refused to tell them my story about the poisoned drink. What if they picked up Swanson and found nothing? Not even the gun?"

"They'd release him, naturally, but—"

"You two met last night at the Golden Slipper, is that right?" Aces asked.

"Yes."

"Did you open your bag while you were there?"

I thought for an instant "No. He paid for my drink, but—"

"Did you open it after you got to his place?"

"No."

Aces pinched his thin lips together thoughtfully. "Is it possible someone other than Swanson could have removed your revolver while you were at the Golden Slipper bar?"

I nodded. "Sure, I guess it's possible. Why?"

Aces gathered up his lanky frame and ambled nervously across the sound stage. "Honey, I'm in a helluva spot. This gun business really scares me. Rod Caine is an expert with a revolver."

"Rod Caine?"

"He's a TV writer—originated the idea of the Bob Swanson show. I fired him several months ago."

"Why?"

"I didn't like him."

"That's all?"

"Not exactly," Aces said grimly. "One night I came home unexpectedly. He was in bed with my wife, Lori."

"That sort of thing does get under one's skin."

"Lori is a very beautiful woman," Aces said, his eyes growing intently dark. "Very beautiful, and very young. She's only twenty. A rare little child. She doesn't know any better. Caine does."

"Where is he now?"

"I don't know. He disappeared. Nobody seems to know where he is. And that's what worries me. I hurt him. Hurt him bad. A cowardly thing. I hit him in the face with a broken glass." He wiped hands over his eyes. "I don't know why exactly. They were lying there, naked and drunk. I grabbed an empty glass from a table beside the bed, shattered it on the metal rim and hit him in the face."

I winced. "How dirty can you get?"

Aces nodded. "I know. There was blood all over the place. I never even saw how bad he was cut. He just put his hands to his face and ran. Nobody's seen him since."

"He must have needed stitches. Did you check the hospitals? His doctor?"

"Sure. He just vanished. Naked, too. The police had no record either."

"Where do you live?"

"Newport. Lido Isle on the bay front."

"Is Caine a good swimmer?"

"I don't know. It was dark as hell. He could have made it to the water. Rain was pouring down and I couldn't follow his trail. But he was bleeding."

"He might be hiding because he's scarred."

"I don't think he's hiding," Aces said tightly. "The incident occurred four months ago. Plenty of time for plastic surgery. I keep wondering if he still has the same features."

"Do you think it was that bad?"

Aces stopped pacing, lit two cigarettes and handed me one. Then he said, "I walk down the street now and look at faces and I ask myself, 'Is that Caine? Where is he? What does he look like?' It drives me crazy. I wonder if he was sitting in the Golden Slipper the night my drink was poisoned. I wonder if he was there last night, if he stole your gun, if—"

"Wait a minute," I interjected. "You forget one thing."

"What's that?"

"If he was bleeding as freely as you say, he might have tired and drifted out to sea."

"I thought about that," Aces said quietly.

"He could be dead."

"Yeah, and if he isn't, the tombstone may be on the other grave. If you know what I mean."

While Meeler and Aces made further script changes, I decided to search the dressing room where I'd left my bag during my appearance the day before. An attractive, green-eyed brunette stopped me just inside the doorway.

"Hi!" she said, much too sweetly. "Remember me?"

"Sure. We met yesterday. You're Ann Claypool, one of the contestants."

"That's right." She flashed me a pasted-on smirk that reeked of bourbon. "I'm the contestant who was supposed to win but didn't. Have you ever heard of a fix that was fixed?"

"I don't think I understand."

"Of course, you wouldn't," she said, weaving slightly. Ann Claypool looked like a grown-up doll with a deep dimple in her cheek, long sweeping eyelashes and a small voluptuous figure. She couldn't have weighed more than a hundred pounds soaking wet.

"You want to know something?" she continued. "I was supposed to have signed that contract you got. It was all decided days ago. Then Sam Aces ruined it. He went and killed it just like he killed my husband!"

"What do you mean?"

"He sent my husband to his death deliberately!"

"How'd he do that?"

Ann Claypool said, "Vince was a specialist in underwater photography. Aces sent him on an impossible assignment." She squinted cynically. "Vince never came back."

I glanced out the window at the mountain of white clouds forming over the blue sky. This case was getting almost as obscure as the distant hills. I shook my head. "Now, look, why would Sam Aces want your husband dead?"

"For revenge," she blurted angrily. "Because I told his wife the truth about him. He was always trying to get me alone in his office. He was always trying to take off my clothes and—well—I told her everything. He said he'd kill me for it. But he killed Vince instead!"

She sat down and put her face in her hands. "Now he's even taken the contract away from me! After he promised!" Her large green eyes looked up and there was a glaze of hate over them. "I'd like to kill him, do you know that? And I'm not the only one. Bob Swanson hates Sam enough to strangle him. And Max Decker feels the same way."

"I don't get this," I said, suspiciously. "Why tell me?"

"Because," Ann snapped drunkenly, "I want you to

know what you're getting yourself into. You think you're pretty smart, don't you? I don't know how you got that contract, but I'm warning you to watch out. Do you understand? You're sitting on a big keg of dynamite and when it blows you're going to be in trouble. Big trouble."

Ann Claypool flashed those hate-filled eyes at me again and walked all too soberly out of the dressing room. I thought about my missing revolver. Could this girl have taken it?

When I saw Aces later in the day I told him how well-liked he was by Ann Claypool and her associates.

"Brother," I sighed. "You're about as popular around these parts as a Russian-made hydrogen bomb."

"Yeah," Aces said, trying to smile. "I guess I should have told you about Vince's death. I was really sorry it happened, believe me. But I wasn't responsible."

"Was she supposed to get the contract?"

"Yeah," Aces said wincing. "I've been trying to give her every break possible. But it doesn't make any difference. I could star her in a three-hour spectacular and she'd still hate my guts."

"Did you really make a play for her?"

"Yeah."

"Did you threaten her after she talked to your wife?"

"Of course I did!" Aces said. "But I was only trying to throw a scare into her. What would you expect me to do? She nearly wrecked my marriage."

I nodded dismally, then added up the credit side of Sam Aces' ledger. Bob Swanson, Ann Claypool, Rod

Caine and possibly Max Decker. Apparently there wasn't a debit anywhere to balance the books.

"What's Max Decker got against you?" I asked, studying the producer as he paced across the sound stage.

"I don't know," Aces said, shaking his head. "I've threatened to take the show to another network several times. Max is a funny guy. To tell the truth, I don't think he likes anyone."

"Sam," I said suddenly, "do you honestly think one of them plans to murder you?"

Aces grinned and put his arm around my shoulder. "I like you, Honey. You have just about everything a woman could want, including brains. Maybe you ought to drop out of this thing before you get hurt."

"If Swanson's our boy," I said, "I'm not worried."

"What about Caine? A butched-up face could go a long way to setting him up for the looney bin. Before I gave him the jagged glass he looked a little like Rock Hudson."

"That's a tough break."

"And if it's Ann Claypool, you're really sitting pretty. You got a contract yesterday she was a cinch to sign. As you said, she's mad as hell about that."

"Swell," I groaned. "Now we're all friends. We ought to throw a big party in Swanson's swimming pool and serve nothing but arsenic-spiked screwdrivers in jagged glasses."

Aces pulled on his coat. "We're leaving for Catalina Island tomorrow aboard my yacht. We'll be filming one of the Swanson shows in and around Avalon and White's Landing. Be gone about four days with the cast and crew. You can make it, of course?"

"Wouldn't miss it for the world. Yachts, Catalina and men are my three favorite sports. This sounds like a Honey West parlay."

"We'll leave around noon. I'm taking my big ship, *Hell's Light*. It's tied up at Wilmington Harbor. Pier Sixty-seven. Just bring a swimsuit and a toothbrush. We'll have plenty of things in wardrobe if you should want to be civilized."

He gave me a copy of the Catalina script. Meeler had already written me in.

"You better start boning up on your lines," Aces grinned, "even if we do have cuing devices. I want to shoot one of your scenes tomorrow."

Great! I didn't have enough on my mind. Now I had to worry about words and speeches and scenes. After Aces left, I stayed in Studio Sixteen wrestling with the script, the puzzle of who hated Aces the most and the question of Herb Nelson's murderer. I could hardly keep them all straight.

I thought about Lori Aces. How did she fit? Was she really in love with her husband? Maybe I could study that situation during the Catalina trip. No doubt, she'd be along. Or would she? Then I got to thinking about Ann Claypool. She had a lot of hate welled up inside of her. But she had such a sweet rhythmic voice. It sounded like woodwinds or flutes.

The big clock on the wall of Stage Sixteen pointed to

ten-thirty. I could hardly keep my eyes open. I got up, stretched and bent over to pick up my purse.

That's when I heard another sound. It was not rhythmic. It was deadly. Bullets have a special sound all their own.

FIVE

I STRAIGHTENED UP QUICKLY AND LUNGED FOR COVER behind a TV camera as a second shot screamed off the side of the metal case. The character with the gun was somewhere in the metal beams above the sound stage. It was a country mile up there, and dark. I couldn't see a soul. A chill went through me. This reminded me of a horror movie I saw years ago, Lon Chaney in *Phantom of the Opera*. There was no telling who was crawling around in the maze of ventilating tubes, light fixtures and pitch blackness.

I waited nervously for the third barrage. It didn't come. There was the sudden sound of a door closing high up in the stage loft and then nothing. My sniper friend evidently had decided to call it quits.

About then I became aware of a sharp pain. I felt around. My hand came up red.

Dr. Carter had just completed his examination of my wound when Lieutenant Mark Storm came striding into

South Bay Emergency. The big detective was followed closely by Fred Sims.

"What the hell's going on, Honey?" Mark demanded. "Hey Doc, I got a report somebody shot at her from behind. What's the damage?"

"The damage," I said angrily, "is in the report. The word *from* is a lie."

"You're kidding," Fred grunted.

"Think so?" I said, touching the back of my skirt gingerly. "If I weren't a lady I'd show you the Band-Aid."

The white-haired medical man crinkled his face slyly. "Just a flesh wound boys, nothing critical."

Fred and Mark, two guys who had pulled me out of more scrapes and tight spots than Dr. Carter had pills, smothered a pair of grins.

"Same old Honey," Mark said pointedly, glancing at the crippled newspaperman. "Always leading with her chin. Only this time she turned around and stuck something else out."

"Doc!" I yelled. "Get-these two nitwits out of here before I commit murder!"

Mark took off his hat, leaned his six-foot-five tower down and stuck his chin out. "All right," he said, "murder me!"

I measured him with my fist, then leaned into his face with my lips. There was something I really liked about this crazy detective. I wasn't certain whether it was his looks, his build or his personality. He had a rugged face with thick black brows, deep, quiet brown eyes and solid massive shoulders that tapered down into an Olympic physique. Mark was a boomeranged mixture of wit, tomfoolery and plain horse-sense.

A piece of finely sanded hickory interrupted us, pushing Mark away from me. "Hey," Fred pleaded, "am I always going to be the other man?"

I grinned, kissed Fred and the three of us walked down to a nearby coffee shop. Immediately they both grew serious. Dead serious. I told them the story of Sam Aces and his "unfriendly" associates.

"Get out of this, Honey!" Mark warned. "There's a real screwball mixed up in it somewhere and he's not going to be satisfied until everybody's got a few extra holes. And I don't mean just from bullets. Arsenic can cut a few capers of its own."

I nodded. "Sure, there're a lot of screwballs mixed up in this case, but I can't tell yet which screwball is the one who murdered Herb Nelson."

At the mention of Herb's name the two men flinched. "Honey," Fred started, "we have something to tell you—"

"Let me tell her," Mark interrupted. He stirred his coffee for an instant and then studied me with the same protective expression on his face that he'd had the night we found Herb's battered body. "Honey, you remember we—we didn't know what sort of instrument had been used on Herb? Well, we've found out. It was the Oscar."

"No," I groaned, "but, we—"

"I know," Mark said. "The killer must have cleaned it in an effort to wipe off fingerprints. The lab says that's definitely what was used."

Fred kept his eyes lowered. "He was so badly battered identification had to be made from rings and clothing and physical structure."

I sagged in my chair. The thought of the brutal murder of Herb Nelson still made me tighten with shock.

"I'm going to bring Swanson in for questioning," Mark said, sipping at his coffee. "I'm anxious to give him a couple of hours under the sweat lamp." He grinned, an expression that was contrary to what he felt inside. "Of course, we'll install an infra-red bulb for Mr. Muscle Man."

I didn't agree on the idea. Swanson would be a tough man to pump. It'd be better to catch him off guard. Maybe aboard Aces' yacht. Liquor did a lot of fancy things with Mr. Swanson's insides. Even took care of the microbes. I asked Mark to lay off for a few more days.

"We're going to Catalina tomorrow," I said. "The ship'll be jammed with partial sets, lights, cast, crew, the works. I don't think he'll pull any tricks."

"I wouldn't bet on it," Mark said.

"What would you bet on?" I asked.

"Murder. Two to one you're going to lose another client, Honey girl. The only way to stop it is haul in Swanson."

"I'll stop it," I said.

"Yeah," Mark finished, "that's what worries me."

Pier Sixty-seven in Wilmington Harbor looked like D-Day on the beach at Normandy. They were loading half of Television Riviera aboard *Hell's Light*. And at least a hundred cases of liquor. The ship wasn't going to be the only thing afloat during this journey.

Hell's Light was the largest private yacht I'd ever seen. It had two decks, three lifeboats and a fantastic circular bar that could seat fifty people. The bar, stools and built-in hi-fi equipment were set squarely in the middle of a swimming pool. To get a drink, it was necessary to swim or wade through the comfortably heated water. Now I knew why Aces had said to bring only a toothbrush and a bathing suit. What else did I need?

The swimming-pool bar was already jammed, still an hour until sailing time. I recognized a few familiar faces and bodies: patch-eyed Golden Boy, crocked to the teeth and wearing a blue denim outfit that was soaked to his skin; Ann Claypool sitting on the bar, singing and not wearing much of anything; Joe Meeler, staring at all his drunken associates as if he wished they were all dead; Sam Aces, decked out in a red jacket and captain's hat that was as cockeyed as he was; and a face and figure that I'd never seen before, but recognized instantly as Lori Aces. She was a rare little child all right, just as Aces had said. Sam claimed she was twenty which made her roughly thirty years his junior. Actually she looked closer to sixteen. Lori was the only one without a drink besides Meeler.

Aces saw me immediately, waved and floundered over. Apparently he wasn't much of a swimmer. In fact, he waded the entire distance. He showed me to my cabin, a big comfortable room well enough forward to provide a view off the ship's bow.

Two incidents were unusual during that trip: the sudden appearance of Max Decker, who was supposed to have missed the boat, and a back-slapping relationship that developed between Sam Aces and Bob Swanson.

We anchored about a half-mile off shore at White's Landing, the summer site of a YMCA camp. A camera crew went ashore to set up for the next day's film sequences. I hitched a ride on the small boat. So did Lori Aces, who seemed disgusted with the chaos aboard *Hell's Light*.

"I think my husband likes that cheap Claypool girl," Lori said. "Did you see the way she kept looping the other half of her lei over the men and hugging them?"

The boat angled up beside the pier. We climbed out, then separated from the camera crew and started up the white beach. I asked Lori if she knew what had ever happened to Rod Caine. She denied knowing the writer until I told her I was a private detective hired by her husband. We talked about the night Aces caught Lori and Caine under the covers.

"I was having a drink," Lori said, "I was lonesome. Sammy works so many nights, you know! Rod came by the house and we had a few martinis. He kissed me a couple of times and then—the next thing I knew we were in bed together."

"He must be some man."

"I guess so," Lori said softly. "I'm only eighteen. I haven't had much experience. In fact, with Sammy it was the first time for me."

Now I knew the age score. About thirty-two years difference between Aces and Lori. A wide gap.

"Have you seen or heard from Caine since that evening?"

"You won't tell my husband, will you?"

"This is strictly between us, I promise."

"He called me about three weeks ago. I asked him where he was, but he wouldn't tell me. He said he was so mad at what Sammy had done, he'd like to kill him."

"How badly was his face injured?"

"He wouldn't tell me a thing, but he did ask me the strangest question." Lori looked puzzled.

"What was that?"

Lori's bathing suit had big buttons down the front and she fiddled with them nervously. "He asked me if Sammy's favorite drink was still a screwdriver."

I winced. "You never told your husband about the phone call?"

"No, I was afraid to. He goes mad with jealousy. Like the night he shoved the glass in Rod's face. I was afraid he might think there was more to it than just the phone call."

"Has Sam ever mentioned Herb Nelson to you?"

"Sure."

"When exactly?"

Lori said, "Lot's of times. Sam felt sorry for Herb. He was always trying to get him into bit parts in the Swanson show, but Bob kept saying no. Bob's one hundred percent louse."

We decided to take a swim. Lori was obviously an

He grinned again. "For my money you're already filled in. And in just the right places."

"Thanks." I felt my cheeks growing hot. "Where am I?"

"In my cabin. On the hill overlooking White's Landing. I was doing a little spear fishing when I found you poking around in my abalone beds."

"Was I alone?"

"Not exactly. There were a couple of wide-eyed fish in the vicinity, but I got there first."

The left side of my jaw felt extremely sore. "You didn't by any chance hit me with a KO punch?"

"Not until you gave me some of the same in the lower intestine. If you want the facts, ma'am, you tossed me one below the belt."

"I'm sorry." Then I suddenly remembered Lori Aces. With her talent for swimming she should easily have maneuvered her ninety-odd pounds to a safe landing place. Maybe even the beach.

He interrupted my train of thought. "How about some coffee?"

"First things first," I said. "How about some clothes?"

"Fresh out of clothes," he teased. "Plenty of coffee."

"How'd you get me here?" I asked, trying to sit up. He pushed me down in a firm, nice manner. "You swallowed a lot of water. I had to carry you up the hill. You weren't about to walk on your own two feet. What were you doing swimming around half naked in the first place?"

"An old custom of mine. It scares the tar out of sharks."

"Great!" he said. "You scared the tar out of me. I thought you were a shark for a few seconds. That is, until I put my arm around your waist."

"And that convinced you?"

"Well, no shark I ever knew had what you've got," he laughed. There was a long silence.

"What's your name?" I asked.

"Ralph—Ralph Smith. What's yours?"

"Honey West."

"The female private eye?"

"You carried me up the hill," I said. "Have you got any doubts about my sex?"

"Not in the least. What are you doing at Catalina?"

"Investigating the buffalo. What's your excuse?"

"I'm writing a novel."

"What's it about?"

Smith walked over to stoke the fire. "That nasty, dirty little business called television."

"You sound as if you know something about the subject."

He was pensive for a moment. "I do. I was around when the first TV show went on the air in Los Angeles."

"Are you still in television?"

"Nope. It got too dirty for me."

"You ever know a writer named Rod Caine?" He bent over the fire and tossed on another log. "Yeah," he said after a pause, "I know him."

"What's he like?"

"Why?"

"He may be working his way to the gas chamber. If he's the sensible type maybe I can warn him off before he kills a client of mine."

Smith stood up, turned and looked at me, half grinning, half serious. "You're kidding! Who's your client?"

I told him the story. He listened attentively, especially when I mentioned the poisoned drink mixed at the Golden Slipper and Lori's disappearance earlier in the huge swell. Smith, expressing concern for her safety, pulled on a raincoat and hat.

"You should have told me there were two of you," he said. "Even if she made shore, she might be battered to pieces in this storm."

He ran out of the cabin and the wind lashed the door shut behind him. It was a furious gale leadened with rain. If Lori hadn't found shelter, her chances for survival in this kind of storm were about as good as a hundred-mile-an-hour approach to a hairpin curve with no warning signs. I wondered how *Hell's Light* was taking the blow. Probably the customers in the swimming-pool bar were so frightened, they were drinking with both hands and getting stiffer than boards. I hoped Sam Aces wasn't too stiff. His kind of stiffness could turn out to be permanent if he didn't keep a weather eye open.

I searched around for some clothes. In the closet was an old pair of white dungarees with the cuffs rolled up. There was quite a space to make up for around the middle, but an old piece of rope helped cinch in the waist A red-striped cotton shirt, minus any buttons, hung on the same hook. I slipped it on and tucked the tails inside the trousers to keep the shirt together.

Smith returned a few minutes later soaked to the skin and breathing heavily. "I slipped on a rock down near the boat cave and went in up to my shoulders," he explained. "Didn't make much difference. I was drenched by that time anyway."

"See anything?"

"Yeah. One of the permanent buildings down on the YMCA site lost part of a roof. Same thing may happen to us if it gets any worse."

I winced. "Nothing of Lori Aces?"

He stripped off his wet shirt. "Maybe she made it to one of the caves at the south end of the beach. She'd be safe there." He knelt before the fire. "How about something to eat? You must be starved!"

"What about yourself?" I studied him carefully. His body was deeply bronzed from the sun. Then I said, "You'd better get out of those wet pants."

He grinned and pulled me down next to him in front of the fireplace.

"I don't take orders from *nobody*," he said quietly. "Especially a female investigator who packs a .32."

"How'd you know I carry a .32?"

"I don't know." He shrugged his shoulders. "A .32 seems about the right caliber for a woman." Then his lips touched mine, and they were warm and soft. He lifted his head finally and whispered, "I told you I was fresh out of clothes. Where'd you get these?"

"In the closet," I said.

He touched the opening at the top of my shirt and kissed me again.

I felt my legs wobble slightly as I forced myself up. "What'll it be? Bacon and eggs, hot cakes, waffles—?" He came after me and his hands pulled me close to him.

"Aren't—aren't you hungry?" I stammered. His mouth kissed the bruise on my chin. "You—must have worked up a big appetite wandering around in the rain—"

"Yeah, I did," he said.

"I'd—better get into the kitchen then—"

His lips moved over my mouth shutting out the words. He picked me up and carried me into the bedroom.

"Look," I said, "I don't even know you—"

Wind suddenly bit furiously into the cabin. The roof trembled and screeched as shingles ripped loose into the stormy sky. One of them hit the bedroom window splintering glass across the room.

He put me on my feet hurriedly, grabbed his slicker and vanished into the night.

I glanced down at the front of my shirt.

The flesh underneath was crimson and I was trembling.

It was still raining when I awakened. The bedroom window had been boarded up, but Ralph Smith was nowhere in view. Wind rustled softly in the distant dark.

In the living room I found him curled up like a big dog in front of the fireplace. I shook my head and crossed into the kitchen. The clock said it was a few minutes after midnight.

The old-fashioned wood stove was all set for a fire. I lit a match to it, started some bacon sizzling in a skillet and looked for a fork. The kitchen drawers were filled with everything except silverware.

I walked into the living room, rummaged around in a desk drawer and came up with a couple of knives and forks. Leave it to a man to keep books and papers in the kitchen and silver in the desk!

Something else in that drawer startled me. A photograph of Lori Aces! Sweet, little, childlike Lori Aces. She got around more than measles. There was a signature on the front of the picture. *I Love You Passionately—Lori.* She obviously was as crazy for Sam Aces as a detonator hooked up to a ton of dynamite. First Rod Caine, now Ralph Smith. No wonder he got excited at the mention of her name.

I shoved the picture back and started toward the kitchen when I saw the bronze statuette of an Emmy, television's equivalent to motion picture's Academy Award Oscar.

The inscription read, *For outstanding achievement in the development and creation of the Bob Swanson Show, WBS Network.*

The winner's name was etched on the face of the plate in fancy letters. *Rod Caine.*

SEVEN

I RAMMED THE STATUETTE DOWN HARD BREAKING A GLASS bowl. The sound brought him to his feet, a startled expression on his face. "What in hell's the matter?" he yelled. "The roof coming off?"

"You can say that again!" I boomed. "The roof, two floors of furniture and the kitchen sink."

He glanced around. "You out of your mind?"

"Yes, I am, *Mr. Caine!*"

The puzzled expression drained out of his handsome face. He took the statuette and placed it back on the shelf. "So, you found out? You've been looking for me, haven't you? Well, here I am!"

"Thanks," I said.

"I suppose I should have told you right away. But I'm not trying to hide anything. Ralph Smith is my *nom de plume.*"

"What?"

"Pen name. Fictitious."

"You mean fake, don't you?" I realized I was shouting. "That's you all over. Just about as fake as they come!"

He shook his head.

"How come no facial scars?" I asked. "Plastic surgery?"

"Some," Caine said. "The wounds weren't as bad as they looked. I was practically healed inside of two weeks."

"Why didn't you go back to Television Riviera?"

"I was fired. Besides, I was glad to be out of there. This new novel's much more important to me. Aces actually did me a favor."

"Now you'd like to return the favor," I said.

"Not the way you think!"

"Did you call Lori three weeks ago and ask if Aces still drinks screwdrivers?"

"Don't be idiotic."

"Did you say you'd like to get Aces for what he did to you?"

"No!" Rod insisted. "I haven't seen or talked to Lori Aces for over four months."

"This is important," I said. "Whose idea was it—the martinis, the kisses, bed?"

"Lori's idea. The whole thing. She invited me up with the understanding Sam was out of town for a couple of days. I was floored when he walked in."

"Imbedded is a better word," I said. "Where'd you go after you ran out?"

"Into the bay."

"Then where?"

"To a small yacht that was anchored about a half mile down from Lori's place. There was a doctor on board. I told him I'd been attacked by something in the water. He stitched me up and that was that."

"No questions about why you were naked?"

"No more than I asked you!" He grinned again. Rod Caine had a most infectious smile.

"How long have you been living on the island?"

"About three months. I moved to Catalina after the plastic surgery, bought this cabin and started working on the novel."

"Have you ever been back to the mainland?"

"Sure. A month later for a final examination of my face."

"Any other time?"

"Two weeks ago. I picked up a few supplies and came right back."

"Did you go to Hollywood?"

Rod hesitated, then said, "Yeah. I wanted to see my agent, but it was too late. He'd already left the office."

"Go any place else?"

He shrugged. "Sure, I stopped for a couple of drinks."

"Where?"

He hesitated again. "The Golden Slipper. That was my old hangout before—"

"Did you see anyone you know?"

Rod laughed half-heartedly. "Are you kidding? You couldn't recognize a Siamese twin in that place, even if it belonged to you."

"What time was it?"

"I don't know!" Rod said harshly. He crossed toward the kitchen, then whirled around. "All right, I did see Swanson. He was sitting at the bar. I talked to him for a few minutes. He was so swacked I doubt if he remembered it afterward. He was taking a drink back to Aces at the studio. I wouldn't have thought a thing about it except Bob kidded me about the broken-glass incident. He said it was lucky I wasn't taking the drink to Sam or I might slip in a little poison to even the score." Rod stopped and wiped his hands over his face. "Hell, that's insane!"

"Maybe," I said. "Have you ever been back to the Golden Slipper since that night?"

"No."

"You're certain?"

"Dammit! Of course, I'm certain."

"Have you been in Television Riviera?"

"No!"

"Not even the day after the last Swanson show?"

"No! What would I be doing there?"

I said quietly, "You originated the show. Doesn't it bother you not to be part of it any more."

Rod shook his head. "Aces gave me a raw deal, sure. Okay. But I never should have been in bed with his wife, so we're even."

"Are you in love with her?"

"If I were, don't you think I'd be out looking for her right now?"

"Depends on what kind of a man you are."

"Try me sometime!"

"I already have. You saved my life. I still haven't thanked you for that."

"You can return the favor by taking me off the hook. I don't want to kill anyone."

I stared at him and in the distance, through one of the windows, lightning touched the dark sea and then disintegrated. I closed my eyes, but the picture clung to my retina like the image of Herb Nelson's body, which was imprinted indelibly upon the mirror of my mind.

"Answer me one thing," I said. "Have you ever worked with Herb Nelson?"

He hesitated for an instant. "Too bad about him, wasn't it? I—I thought he was one tremendous actor. No, I never worked with him on anything. I only wish I had. The last I saw or heard of Herb Nelson, he was working as a bartender's assistant at the Golden Slipper."

"What time is it?"

Rod peered at the kitchen clock. "Twelve-thirty."

"Have you got a boat?"

"Sure," Rod said. "I got a boat. What about it?"

"Could you get us out to *Hell's Light*?"

He did a double-take and then grinned. "Are you kidding? In this storm? We wouldn't stand a chance."

"Sounds as if the wind's eased up."

Rod walked outside to check the weather. I knew I'd better get back to the ship as soon as possible. In all the confusion of wind, rain and whiskey, Sam Aces stood a good chance of getting what someone had been trying to give him for several weeks. A lesson in not breathing!

Rod came in from his weather inspection. "You're right," he said. "The wind's down considerably. So's the water. I think we can make the yacht if you want to try."

"What are we waiting for? Let's go!"

We dressed warmly and started down the face of the hill toward the water. Rain sifted through a sky cross-patched with thick black clouds and intermittent stars. His boat, a small cabin cruiser, was stored in a deep ocean cave below the house. Rod lowered her into the water by pulley and cable and we climbed aboard, nearly being thrown into the water, as a big wave smashed into the cave. It took a few minutes to navigate out into the open sea, then we turned toward the faint, distant lights of Aces' floating funland.

Waves, blown gayly by the wind, crested over our bow, but Rod kept the cruiser straight on course. We approached the yacht from the stern. She was impressive in the storm, her gleaming white sides sloping up into the dark sky. Somebody lowered the landing for us.

It was wild, but between Rod and several of the yacht's crew, they managed to secure the boat and raise her up out of the water. The float was lifted again.

The swimming-pool bar was jammed. We didn't even make a dent in the mad conglomeration. Max Decker, flushed, filled and fat, squandered his weighty load on two bar stools, spilling over both. Ann Claypool was providing most of the entertainment with a rock-and-roll version of the bump and grind.

Ann was dancing on top of the bar and her wiggle was a smash hit. All she wore was a blue denim yachting cap. The headdress looked familiar. It had the word CAPTAIN sewn across the front. Sam Aces had been wearing that cap earlier, but there was no sign of the producer. There was no sign of Bob Swanson either.

Joe Meeler seemed to be the only sober one in the place. I asked him about Aces.

"Last thing I know," Joe said, trying to talk above the din, "Swanson and Aces took off for a little stroll around the deck. Lord, you woulda' thought they were a couple of queers, they were so palsy-walsy."

"Have you seen Lori Aces?" I asked.

"Sure," Joe said. "She came back with the camera crew late this afternoon. They had one helluva time in this storm, believe you me."

When I got back to the edge of the pool, even Rod Caine was gone. I started for Aces' cabin. This looked bad. Swanson was out for a promenade with Sam while Rod Caine was rendezvousing with Lori.

I suddenly felt as ridiculous as a jockey seeing his horse break from the starting gate and finding with horror he's still in the chute.

I banged on the producer's cabin door. There were no lights on inside and the door was locked. I ran forward, hammering on doors, trying knobs. One opened and I entered hurriedly. The bed was occupied by two-bit players scrambled together like two crisp pieces of bacon fried into an egg. They didn't even look up. I raced out. The wind was rising again and so was the sea. Whitecaps crackled in the churning water below. I wondered if Sam Aces were down there.

There was a light in my cabin. I opened the door. Aces was sprawled across my bed, legs and arms hanging limply over each side. My heart sank to my knees. I stepped inside and slammed the door.

Aces sat up, stretched, yawned and peered at me. "Where you been, Honey?" he asked. "I been worried about you."

"Sam, I thought you were dead! Where's Swanson?"

"You got me," Aces said, grinding to his feet. "We got to be as thick as thieves in the bar. Then he suggested we take a walk. I didn't like the sound of that, but I went along. When we got out on deck, I don't know whether it was the ship pitching or old B. S. pushing, but I damn near went over the railing. That's when we quit being friends."

"How'd you get in here?"

Aces tried to shake some of the whiskey out of his cranium. "I don't know exactly. I remembered your gun and that's about all I remember until now. What time is it, anyway?"

"About two o'clock."

"How'd you get back to the ship?"

I told him the whole story, including the part about Lori's picture in Rod Caine's drawer.

"You mean that son-of-a-B is aboard my ship?" Aces roared.

"Someplace," I said. "I lost him in the shuffle. But I got a hunch where we might find him."

We headed for the swimming pool. Wind and rain swept the decks wildly, pushing us around like paper dolls. Rod was sitting at the bar with Lori.

Aces waded over with me and grabbed Rod by the arm.

"Get out of here, Caine! Get off this ship before I throw you off!"

Rod didn't ruffle a feather. He gently lifted Sam's hand away and said, "Now, that isn't being very hospitable, is it, Mr. Aces? Is that all the thanks I get for bringing your blonde bombshell back to her base?"

"Don't do me any favors, Caine. I don't need your kind of help. Now get out of here!"

Lori tried to intercede. "Sammy, please! Rod saved Miss West's life. Let's let bygones be bygones."

"No!" Aces roared.

His voice barely caused a ripple in the noise and confusion. Ann Claypool, still dancing and singing on the bar, was shouting her lungs out. And beyond, in the wet darkness, the storm was creating its own impossible clamor.

Rod grinned, his usual grin, and quietly mixed Aces a drink. Then Swanson appeared out of nowhere, breasting the water in his inimitable muscular style. He looked at Caine, then at Aces and exploded wildly.

"Let me at him!" he roared. "Let me at Caine! I'll kill the bastard!"

He flailed and stumbled around drunkenly but never even got close to Rod Caine. Sam Aces intervened with a smashing blow to Swanson's mouth that caught the muscle man completely offguard. He stood for an instant, eyes widened, blood spilling from the wound, then slowly submerged in the water of the swimming pool. Rod helped me drag him to the side of the pool.

"What is this?" I said to Caine. "You and Swanson were supposed to be pals. What happened the night in the Golden Slipper that you haven't told me about?"

Rod shook his head. "Nothing. I told you everything. Now forget it!"

I shook my head angrily. Rod Caine wasn't telling me half what he knew. Had he seen Swanson put something in Aces' drink? Or was it the other way around? Or was it that everyone had a hankering to hang one on the capricious Mr. Caine's jaw? But the biggest riddle was why Sam Aces suddenly stepped in between the two and lowered the boom on Golden Boy.

Swanson was all out of the fighting mood when he came to his senses. He growled a few times and skulked off to his cabin. Rod was about to head back to the beach when things really went haywire.

Aces stopped him. "I'm sorry I flew off the handle, Caine. Why not stay the night? You'll have a tough time making shore the way the storm's going now."

Rod accepted gratefully. We joined Lori at the bar again and immediately Decker floated over. There was one thing about Max Decker. Drunk or sober, he didn't have to shout to be heard.

"Good to see you again, Rodney," he bellowed, pumping Caine's hand. "I thought maybe you were dead."

This time it was Rod's turn to get nasty. He didn't hit Decker, but he might as well have. He gave the big man one of the roughest five minutes on record. When it was over, everyone seemed willing to call it a night, but we got naked little Annie instead. She obviously knew Rod Caine well.

She flopped into his lap. "Hi, honey man! I been missing you, where you been?"

"In a clothing store," Rod quipped. *"Why don't you try one for size?"*

"Now, sweetie," Ann said drunkenly, "when the public clamors, you got to give them what they want. Isn't that right, Sam boy?"

Before Sam Aces had a chance to answer, Lori cried, "Can it, Claypool! Can it and sell it on Main Street where you can make yourself a buck."

The two gals were about the same size and weight. I thought for a second they'd square off in another fight but they never had a chance to get up out of their corners.

Sam Aces suddenly turned green, grabbed his throat and screamed as if he'd just swallowed a pint of broken glass.

The bar patrons stopped dead in their drunken tracks. Aces lurched through the water toward me with a tall orange drink in his hand and as I tried to catch him, he went down. I got the drink instead.

While I juggled the glass, Aces sank and came up again, still screaming, still off balance. Several people tried to stop him, but failed in their efforts. He crawled up the side of the pool, staggered, fell and got up again, finally disappearing onto the storm-drenched upper deck.

"He's poisoned!" someone yelled.

Rod Caine ditched Ann in the pool and came after me. Apparently he wanted Sam's glass, but I wasn't about to give it up.

Clutching the glass firmly, I waded to the edge of the pool and started after Aces. Caine was hot on my heels. So were a few others, including Decker, Meeler, Ann Claypool and Lori Aces.

If there was poison in the glass, I had to get the contents to a safe place. More important, I had to find Aces and dig up an antidote in a hurry.

A light burned in a cabin up ahead. I recognized it as Aces' and turned in. The bit players were gone. I went into the bathroom, opened the cabinet and took down a small ceramic figurine used for storing old razor blades. The container was almost empty.

I shook out the blades and poured the contents of Aces' glass into the narrow slot. Replacing the piece of pottery, I noticed a bottle of orange-colored medicine bearing the label, *Suspension Co-Pyronil Antihistamine.* It looked like concentrated orange juice. A bright thought struck me. I poured a small quantity of the thick liquid into Aces' glass and added water. What a break! It looked enough like the original contents of the glass to fool anyone.

Suddenly the cabin was swarming with people. Caine extracted the glass from my hand and grinned.

"I'll take care of this," he said. "I can analyze it at my place tomorrow. I've got lab equipment there." Lori stood behind Rod.

"'Remind me to analyze you sometime, Mr. Caine,'" I said. "Especially if we find Sam Aces dead."

We split up and searched *Hell's Light*. The wind, rain and darkness made it difficult. I finally tried my own cabin. The door was banging loudly in the wind and it was pitch dark inside.

The hair on the back of my neck began to twitch. And with good reason. Something was hanging from the ceiling. A rope with a body attached to it. Caine appeared behind me in the open doorway, a flashlight in his hand.

"What's the matter?" he shouted over the roar of the storm.

I didn't have to answer. The flashlight beam caught the round white face under the rope. It was Bob Swanson.

EIGHT

I SWITCHED ON THE CABIN LIGHT. GOLDEN BOY WAS hanging from a rope looped through a metal ring in the ceiling. The cord was hooked under his arms. We lifted him down.

"What the hell do you make of this?" Rod peered at me through narrowed eyes.

I examined Swanson's head. "Big lump, here, over his right temple. He must have been struck by a pretty solid object."

Swanson began to make sounds. He opened his eyes and looked at us. "What hit me?"

I grinned. "From the looks of the lump, I'd say the Twentieth Century Limited. Where'd this happen?"

He looked about the room dazedly. "Right here. I was going through some of your drawers."

"What for?" I demanded.

"Your gun," Golden Boy grunted. "I knew you had

one. Lori told me you did. I wanted to find it so I could blow his brains out."

"Whose brains?" Rod asked.

"Aces'! That dirty bastard!" Swanson tried to get up. "I'll kill him, so help me, I'll kill him!"

"You wanted to do the same thing to Rod Caine twenty minutes ago," I said. "What is it with you, anyway?"

Swanson felt the lump over his right ear. "Caine knows why I said that to him. That's not important now. Aces is. He's hit me for the first and last time. When I see him I'm going to put a hole right through his middle."

"Who do you think jumped you in here?" I asked. "Did you see or hear anything?"

Golden Boy grimaced. "No. I was bent over. There was a lot of noise outside from the storm. I didn't even hear the door open."

"Serves you right for going through a lady's drawers," I said. "Did you find the gun?"

"Do you think I'd still be here if I had?" Swanson tried to stand up, but his legs were like rubber.

I gazed about the room. A chair was overturned a few feet from where the rope dangled from the ceiling. Then I spotted a piece of pipe lying under the edge of the bed. I picked it up in a small towel and showed the weapon to Caine.

"Half-inch," Rod said quickly. "Looks like a fitting for a gas or steam line."

Swanson grabbed the pipe before I could stop him. "So that's what hit me! Wonder it didn't crush my skull."

"I'll go along with that," I said angrily. "With as few brains as you've got I'm surprised you weren't flattened right down to your oxfords."

"What do you mean by that crack?" he howled.

"If you hadn't smeared your fingerprints all over the weapon, we might have found your friend."

Golden Boy groaned, touched the patch on his eye and said, "This is all your fault! Everything's gone wrong since we hired you!" He staggered through the door into the drenching rain.

Rod helped me search the yacht but we found no trace of Sam Aces. About four o'clock we checked the bar again. Everybody had gone to bed.

Exhausted, I slumped clown on the edge of the pool and glanced at the weary-eyed writer. "Well, what do you think?"

"Maybe it's all a joke," Rod said, stretching his arms. "We're not absolutely certain there's poison in that glass. Maybe he took one of his own small boats."

"None of the boats are missing."

"Okay," Rod continued. "Maybe he swam to shore."

"Very funny!"

"He was drunk. Maybe he carried his joke too far."

"Listen," I said. "I don't care how drunk he was, nobody would go into the water during a storm like this."

"A good swimmer might. I've seen a lot of fools attempt it."

"Not Sam Aces," I insisted. "He can't swim a stroke."

"How do you know that?"

"I watched him earlier. There's only one way he'd have gone into that ocean peacefully—and that's dead!"

Rod scanned the swimming-pool area. "All right," he said, "let's assume he's dead. That he was poisoned and thrown overboard. Who slipped him the arsenic?"

"Any number of people could have, not excluding present company."

He smiled. "Thanks for the compliment. Maybe you figure I was the one who slugged Swanson and hung him from the ceiling, too?"

"It's possible."

"Now wait a minute," he argued. "I was in the bar with you and the others when Aces staggered out. I couldn't have been in your cabin at the same time."

"You forgot," I reminded tightly. "We searched for Sam about twenty minutes before discovering Swanson in my cabin. That was plenty of time for you or anyone to string him to the ceiling."

Rod threw his hands up in a mock pretense of surrender. "You got me, pal."

"I didn't say you did it."

"Then who do you think did it?"

"Could be Bob Swanson."

"What?" Rod stared at me for a moment. "Are you kidding? I suppose Bob knocked himself out, then strung up the rope, took a running jump, leaped into the noose and at the same time pushed the poisoned body of Sam Aces overboard."

"Nope," I said. "Maybe Swanson poisoned Aces' drink in the wild melee at the bar, then waited outside

on deck and hurled Sam over the railing when he came
outside—"

"Now wait a minute—"

"Afterward he could have gone to my cabin and
fixed a noose, stood up on a chair, slipped his arms
through the loop and pushed the chair away as he hit
himself with the pipe."

"May I say something?"

"Sure, go ahead."

"Nobody in his right mind would take the chance of
fracturing his own skull."

"It's quite possible Bob Swanson is not in his right
mind."

"It's a cinch somebody isn't," Rod agreed. "I'm beginning to wonder about you. Why would a beautiful gal
get involved in this kind of business anyway?"

I brushed a few wet strands of hair away from my
forehead and looked at him. "I was brought up in this
business. My dad was a private detective."

"What do you mean was?"

"Six years ago he was murdered in an alley behind
the Paramount Theater in L.A. I hired myself to find the
killer."

"So you found him, brought him to justice and decided to keep on going in the private-eye game!"

I shook my head. "No. I've never found him—but I
will some day."

"I believe that," Rod said quietly. He handed me a
cigarette. "You asked me about Herb Nelson earlier.
Was he by any chance a client of yours?"

"Yes." I glanced at Rod out of the corner of my eye. "I know what you're thinking. I haven't been doing too well lately, especially if Sam is—"

Rod grunted. "Honey, have you ever considered the idea that Aces might have been poisoned earlier?"

"Sure. Depending upon the amount, you can never tell how long arsenic will take to do its dirty work."

"Have you thought also of the possibility—if Aces is dead—that you'll never find his body?"

"No," I said. "I never thought of that."

"Well, baby, if he went overboard in this storm and was already dead, it may take years to find his body. Maybe it never will turn up."

I didn't like the way he said that. It sounded too positive.

"Why did you take Aces' glass?" I demanded.

Rod glanced at me and smiled. "I knew it would be safe in my possession. If you'd kept that drink I have a feeling someone would have been after you with blood in his eyes."

"You're taking the same chance."

"I'll risk it." He got up, said good night, and left for his cabin aboard the yacht.

After a few minutes I went out on deck. The storm still slashed at the darkness, ripping it intermittently with crooked orange daggers. *Hell's Light* rolled and pitched with new vigor. It was difficult making my way to the bow and I fell several times, once nearly going over the side, and almost losing the oversize dungarees Rod had loaned me.

I came to a large wooden chest anchored to the bow deck. It was big enough to store a body, if anyone had such inclinations. Gripping the heavy lid with both hands, I swung the chest open. Darkness shrouded its contents.

Suddenly the chest became illuminated by a faint circle of light.

Rod Caine stood over me. "What gives?" he said. "I thought you went to bed."

"Give me that flashlight" I probed inside the trunk with the beam. "Would you recognize blood stains if you saw them?"

He nodded slowly.

The faint light, dimmed considerably by the night mist, touched two dark pools which were drying on the bottom of the chest

Rod swore. I couldn't tell whether it was in anger or from surprise.

"How in the devil did that get there?" he demanded.

"I'm sure they weren't left by the Easter Bunny."

'But Aces wasn't bleeding!" Rod protested.

"How. do we know," I said. "We haven't seen him for over two hours."

Rod's face was grim. "I thought sure this thing was all a joke. You know, like in a comedy. You open a closet and out jumps Aces laughing like mad."

I looked at the blood spots again. "Losing much of this stuff leaves a body any way but laughing."

We went to my cabin. The noose still hung from the ceiling. Rod took it down. I watched him carefully. Here was a guy who'd helped me out of a hazardous situation, yet I didn't trust him. I checked to see whether my .32 was still in its hiding place.

The revolver was there, but it was wet. I flipped open the cylinder. Another bullet was gone.

"Tell me something, Rod," I said, holding up my gun. "Are you in cahoots with Lori Aces?"

"Don't be silly."

"There's another bullet missing from my revolver. Lori and Sam Aces were the only ones who saw where I hid the gun. Now what were you doing up on the bow of this ship a few minutes ago? You'd already said good night."

"Looking for Aces. What do you think?"

"I don't know," I slammed angrily. "As dark as it was, and with all the trouble I had getting up there, it would have been possible for you to take the starboard passageway, reach the bow before I did, lift Aces' body out of that trunk and dispose of it somewhere else."

"You're out of your mind!"

"You knew I had a .32 revolver," I argued.

"That's crazy!"

"You also knew who I was before I ever told you."

"You're way out, baby, way out."

"Why don't you like Max Decker?"

"Because he's a big slob and I wouldn't trust him as far as I could throw him. Which is about nothing minus nowhere."

"Why don't you trust him?" I demanded.

"Because," Rod countered, "he's a four-carat, no-good bastard. He hates everything and everybody. If he can't get what he wants, he'll kill it so nobody else can have it. He's tried to crush me several times in my career."

"Did Decker like Aces?"

"It was a screwy relationship. Sometimes Max was so kissing sweet to Sam he would drip with good fellowship. Times like that made me wonder if Aces had something big on the old man."

"Blackmail?"

"Yeah!"

I thought about that. Aces had hired me to track down a poisoner. Two days ago I had agreed with his choice of Swanson and suggested bringing in the police, but Aces had declined fearfully. Had, he been afraid of the police? Blackmailers usually are.

After Rod left, I sat up until daybreak thinking about the cast of characters aboard the good ship *H.L.* One of them was lying and I had a pretty good idea who it was.

Around noon, a few hours after the sun sliced through the dull sky, Lieutenant Mark Storm arrived aboard *Hell's Light*. He looked tired and his shoulders drooped slightly as he walked up the steps from the float.

"I got your message, Honey," he said wearily. "What gives? Has Aces checked out or not?"

I showed him the two blood stains in the bottom of the chest and then filled him in on the details of Aces' disappearance.

"I took the remains of his drink into Avalon this morning and had it analyzed," I said. "It was loaded with arsenic."

"You're positive?"

"Of course I'm positive. I wouldn't have called you if the test had shown plain vodka and orange juice."

Mark scratched his head. "All right, let's talk to a few people. Especially this guy, Swanson."

"He's on the beach right now at White's Landing," I said, pointing toward shore. "So are most of the others. They're going ahead on their shooting schedule for the next show."

"Without Aces?" Mark demanded.

I explained, "He's the producer. Swanson does most of the directing. In fact, he claims he can get along very nicely without Aces."

"I'll bet," Mark said. "Where's Mrs. Producer?"

"She went with Rod Caine to his place to analyze the phony contents of Aces' glass—an orange-colored anti-histamine solution. They still don't know I switched drinks."

"This should be interesting. What if they return with the report that the supposed vodka and orange juice was unadulterated?"

"In that case, I think you can make an arrest." Mark shook his head decisively. "We've got to have a body, Honey. You know that. We don't stand a Chinaman's chance without a body."

"Okay," I suggested. "Lets find one."

We scoured the ship. Down in the engine room we

talked with an old beetle-browed sailor named Carruthers. He told us someone had been below deck during the night going through some tool boxes.

"Was his name Swanson?" I asked. "What did he look like?"

"Couldn't tell you his name," Carruthers said, "Husky critter, though, with a baby face—I remember that."

"Don't you ever watch television?" Mark inquired.

"Nope—never," the old man answered.

We went back up to my cabin. Mark looked at the piece of pipe used on Swanson. He thought the business with the rope sounded pretty ridiculous, but not incriminating.

"You can't hang a man for that," Mark said.

"Don't be funny!"

"What about this Claypool dame?"

"Cute. Maybe too cute. She hates Aces' guts."

"You say she was prancing around in her birthday suit most of the evening?"

"Except for Aces' yachting cap."

"What happened to the cap?"

"I wouldn't know. I imagine it wound up in her cabin."

"Let's take a look," Mark said, going to the door. "We just might find something in the lining."

"What?" I asked.

"Traces of arsenic, baby. That stuff's got to be hidden somewhere."

Ann Claypool's cabin was near the swimming-pool

bar, next to Aces' stateroom. We had been there before, but hadn't noticed the yachting cap. It was no place in sight and even after a thorough search we couldn't find it.

A few minutes later, back at the swimming pool, Mark spotted the cap submerged in a few feet of water.

"That's that," he said. "There's nothing left in this lining, not even the label."

Mark had brought a few changes of clothing from my apartment. I was happy to get into a snug comfortable swimsuit after wearing Rod's battered shirt and sloppy dungarees for the past twelve hours. About this time, Rod and Lori returned to the yacht, grim-faced and tense. Rod studied me angrily.

"No arsenic," he said. "Not one-fiftieth of a milligram."

"Just plain screwdriver?" I asked.

"Not so plain," Rod answered. "I think it was some kind of medicine. A pretty unusual drink for Sam Aces, wouldn't you say?"

"I switched glasses on you," I admitted.

"That was a dirty trick! You should have told me. I went to a lot of trouble!" Rod snapped.

I glanced at Lori. "That's too bad. Aces' drink contained more than four grains of white arsenic. Enough to kill two guys the size of Max Decker."

Lori swallowed enough air to last her a week.

Rod shook his head in amazement.

Decker came out of his cabin, a big smile creasing his jowls. It was a dirty sort of smile that I felt like wiping with the flat of my hand to see if it might come clean.

"Good morning," he roared cheerily. "Lori, I want to thank you for your hospitality, but now I must take my leave. My own yacht is anchored in Avalon Harbor. I'm joining some of the New York network people who are on board. Thank Sam for me when you see him."

"He may be too dead to thank," I said.

"Oh, Miss West," Decker continued, as if he hadn't heard me. "I had a chat with Mr. Swanson this morning and we have decided to dispense with your acting services on the Bob Swanson show. You have been replaced by Miss Claypool."

"What about my six-week contract?" I said angrily. "You can't fire me. I signed a legitimate agreement with Sam Aces."

Decker laughed awkwardly. "Your contract will be honored, naturally. Four hundred a week for six weeks, wasn't that the arrangement?"

I nodded. "I have a copy of the contract in my cabin." Decker continued to carry on like the cat who ate an entire aviary. "You stop by my office next week. A check for twenty-four hundred will be waiting for you. Good day."

Mark brought the fat man to a halt. "Mr. Decker, my name is Storm. L.A. Sheriff's office, homicide bureau."

"What are you doing here?" Decker demanded.

"A large quantity of arsenic was found in Sam Aces' drink. We have a strong suspicion your producer is dead."

"Impossible! Sam'd never pull a trick like that!"

"I didn't say it was suicide," Mark snarled.

"You mean someone murdered him?"

"You're on the right track," I said. "Maybe two some-ones."

Mark studied the big television magnate. "Yours was the only stateroom we were unable to search this morning."

"Well, I was still sleeping when you knocked," Decker said, losing most of his gaiety. "You can check it now if you like; I'm all packed and moved out. In fact, my bags are being loaded aboard a water taxi now."

Mark bolted for the landing float. He took the steps three at a time. In the side pocket of the first suitcase he opened Mark found what he was looking for—a small package of white powder.

NINE

MARK SHOWED THE CONTENTS OF THE PACKAGE TO Decker. "New brand of tooth powder?" he asked.

"Never saw that before," Decker said. "Was it in my luggage?"

"That's right," Mark said. "Can you explain how this quantity of arsenic happens to be in your possession?"

Decker appeared baffled. "Why, no, I can't."

"You're sure?"

"Absolutely. I wouldn't lie!"

I studied the big-bellied emperor of television. He was in a tight spot, and he knew it. If Sam Aces turned up with a stomach full of that powder, not all the TV in Chinatown could save the lord of WBS. But, for a moment, there was no corpse. That made a big difference.

Mark signaled for one of the crew of *Hell's Light* to bring Decker's luggage back aboard ship. "You're going to have to stick around awhile," Mark said.

"You can't hold me!" Decker said hoarsely. "I could have your badge in five minutes."

"I didn't say I was holding you, Mr. Decker. It's just that in the absence of your host, Sam Aces, I'm holding a little party, and I would become very unhappy if any of my guests should refuse to attend."

Decker stomped angrily back to his stateroom. Mark took my hand and we started down to the float.

"Where're we going?" I demanded.

"Out looking for a body," he said. "Dead or alive, we've got to find Sam Aces."

A blue sky stretched cloudlessly over the water as Mark and I climbed aboard a small cabin cruiser he'd borrowed from the chief of the Avalon Police Department. We spent the afternoon searching in deep water and along a sharply irregular shoreline. We found no trace of Sam Aces.

About an hour before sundown we doubled back to White's Landing. Mark noticed the ocean cave below Rod Caine's cabin.

"Let's take a look in there," he said. "Never can tell where a body'll wind up."

We steered the boat inside. Rod's cruiser was gone.

"He's probably still out aboard *Hell's Light*," I guessed. "Let's check the cabin."

Mark tied the cruiser, *Clementine*, to the dock and we trudged up the winding path. The door was unlocked, so we helped ourselves to the invitation and entered. Nothing much had changed since I'd been there. A few more dishes in the sink. A few more ashes in the trays. The bed covers wildly thrown back.

We searched for the lab equipment but found nothing except Aces' glass. It still contained a small amount of the antihistamine. And something new had been added. A lipstick stain on the rim.

Mark examined the lip print. "Was this on the glass last night when you gave it to Caine?"

I shook my head decisively.

Mark held the glass up to the light. The remaining liquid had turned a vivid orange. "It's possible Caine caught on to the switch without putting the contents through a lab test."

'What does that mean?"

"He could have tasted some of it," Mark said.

"You think he figured the drink never contained poison?"

"Either that or he knew it was loaded with arsenic, invited Mrs. Aces back here to examine it with him, gave it a clean bill of health and suggested that she try some."

"Intending to murder her?"

"That's right," Mark said. "Then, when Mrs. Aces laughed, instead of pitching over on her face, and said it tasted like medicine, Caine grabbed the glass and gulped some himself. That's when he guessed what you pulled in that bathroom."

"Rod Caine wouldn't do a thing like that!"

"Are you kidding, Honey? If those two are in a murder plot together, Caine'd do anything to prevent her from implicating him."

We searched Rod's closet and found a typed note in the pocket of his suit coat.

CAINE: MEET ME ABOARD MY YACHT WEDNESDAY NIGHT. WE'LL ANCHOR OFF WHITE'S LANDING. I MAY ACT ANGRY IF ANYONE IS AROUND BUT DON'T LET THAT UPSET YOU. I HAVE AN IMPORTANT PROPOSITION I'M SURE WILL INTEREST YOU. SAM ACES.

There was also a faint penciled notation at the bottom which read: Little Harbor.

"Wednesday was last night," I said. "The night Aces disappeared. Caine never said he had an appointment with Aces!"

"Where's Little Harbor?" Mark demanded.

"On the other side of the island," I explained. "It's desolate. Nothing but rocks and beach. I hiked over Mt. Orizaba once to get there."

"Nice place to bury a body?"

"Lovely. Nobody'd find it in a million years without a detailed map and an oversize crane. Even then I wouldn't bank on it."

Mark studied the piece of paper. "What time did Caine and Mrs. Aces leave *Hell's Light* this morning?"

"About eight o'clock. They were gone almost four hours."

"Did you check Caine's boat after finding those blood stains in the chest?"

"No," I said. "I'd searched it twice earlier. I didn't

think there was any reason— You don't believe Rod Caine moved Aces body from the chest to his boat while I was on my way to the bow?"

"It's possible."

"That's ridiculous," I said. "Then you figure Aces' body was aboard Rod's boat this morning when he left with Lori."

"Right." Mark slapped the note. "I also wonder if Mr. Sam Aces isn't buried at Little Harbor."

I threw my hands in the air. "Do you mind if I present my theory?"

"Why not?"

"I think we're barking up the wrong tree."

Mark said, "What do you mean by that?"

"I mean someone is leading us around like we've got rings in our noses. I don't even think Sam Aces is dead."

Mark brought his hands to his face in a quick, resigned gesture of *here we go again!* He said, "Four grains of arsenic in a man's drink, another bullet missing from your gun, blood stains in a deck trunk, and you come up with the straight-faced opinion you don't think Sam Aces is dead."

"I thought he was until you found that arsenic in Decker's suitcase—then I changed my mind."

"A woman's prerogative," Mark said resignedly. "What wrought this great change?"

"Max Decker's expression when you showed him that poison. He was telling the truth. He didn't have any more idea of how that stuff got there than the man in the moon."

"You're sure of this?" Mark said with a tinge of sarcasm in his voice.

"As sure as I am that I caught Sam Aces in my office looking for the threatening letter which had been sent to Herb Nelson."

"What?"

"He told me he was hiding in my office because someone had followed him from L.A. I believed his story at the time, especially after I checked with a Beverly Hills lab and they verified a previous poison dose brought in by Aces. But I don't know. Something's phony about this guy, Mark. He doesn't ring true—the way he was so afraid and yet he wouldn't go to the police, the way I caught him in my office, the way he hired me to help him and then suggested I quit because I might get hurt. Even the poisoned drink—the way he handed it to me in the bar—the way he ran out before anyone could get to him. To me, these things only add up to an amateur trying to act like a pro and getting away with it because of good breaks.

Mark studied my face. "Are you trying to say Sam Aces killed Herb Nelson, that he was in your office looking for a letter which might have implicated him in the crime, and that now he's trying to confuse everyone into thinking he's dead?"

"Something like that," I said faintly. "I know it sounds weird—"

"Weird?" Mark roared. "It sounds positively absurd. You expect me to believe Sam Aces left some of his own blood in a trunk aboard Hell's Light, planted arsenic in

Decker's luggage, and also in his own glass, slipped this note into Rod Caine's pocket, stole your gun, took two shots at you, hung Swanson from the rafters—"

"All right," I interrupted.

"This would be the greatest one-man act in history—"

"I still don't think he's dead."

"Want to bet?" Mark extended his hand.

I hesitated, then accepted the challenge. Sam Aces had to be alive. He was not the kind of man to die without a struggle.

Stars blazed over Little Harbor as Mark headed the cruiser toward shore. The sea was calm, unusually calm for the windward side of the island, and a bright full moon illuminated the water.

We had used the cruiser's searchlight intermittently in our trip around the northern tip of Catalina. Once to identify a dark object which turned out to be a floating log, and again to intrigue a few flying fish out of their depths. But no Aces!

For two hours we toured the smooth sea outside Little Harbor, carefully avoiding treacherous reefs that sometimes lurked a few inches under water.

I shook my head. "If we keep fooling around in this place, there'll be two bodies floating around for sure. Us."

"Let's anchor and swim to shore," Mark suggested. "It's light enough. Maybe we'll come up with some kind of lead."

He stripped to his swim trunks, fastened a flashlight to his waist and we plunged in.

The reefs were impossible. A jagged coral edge tore a gaping hole in my suit. Mark was raked by a row of greenish needles, which ripped off the flashlight and gashed his leg. Then we got mixed up in thunderous breakers that were ten feet high and weighed a ton. They bounced us both on the beach like a pair of dice on a crap table. When Mark crawled over, I breathlessly lauded him for the most sensational bit of inventive thinking since dynamite.

"How did I know it'd be that rough?" He examined the slash in his leg. "The water was like mush out there around the boat. But it's high tide. The breakers'll simmer down in a couple of hours."

"I hope so," I said as I looked toward the shoreline. A dark shape was stretched out about a dozen yards away on the sand.

"Look!" I pointed.

Mark got to his feet slowly. "You stay here!"

"Why?"

"If it's Aces, he won't look his Sunday best."

"Well, I wouldn't exactly pass as a princess," I said. "Besides, it's probably seaweed."

We crossed the beach and discovered it was seaweed. But a few feet away, illuminated by the moon, was a wet crumpled piece of clothing under a rock ledge. A red jacket The initials S.A. were stitched boldly under the left breast pocket and below the initials we found something else—a bullet hole and an ugly dark blood stain!

TEN

"**N**OW WHAT DO YOU THINK?" MARK DEMANDED. "You recognize this jacket?"

I nodded slowly. "Sam was wearing it the last time I saw him in the bar, but—"

"You still don't think he's dead?"

"I didn't say that."

"That's what I thought." The lieutenant, clutching the jacket in his hand, limped up the beach a few yards. When he returned, he said, "This'll do until a body comes along. We'll check these blood stains with the ones in the bottom of that chest. I think they'll match."

"And where do you imagine Sam Aces is now?"

Mark looked out at the thrashing breakers and the needle-sharp reef beyond. "There," he said. "Probably caught below the surface in one of the caverns. The jacket must have floated to the top and was washed in by the heavy surf."

"Maybe," I said. "But until we find a body all bets are off."

"We'll find him."

"How?"

"After daybreak when the tide's down, I'll—"

Suddenly, the sound of the cruiser's engines starting up hoarsely in the tiny bay, attracted our attention. Clouds of vapor boiled up from the twin exhausts and quickly the cabin cruiser whirled around shooting up a curtain of spray. Before we could let out a protest, it vanished in the inky darkness of the open sea.

It seemed an eternity before we could find words to replace our surprise. Half joking, half bewildered by the sudden turn of events, I whispered, "Don't—don't tell me your corpse came up out of the reef?"

"We had a stowaway," Mark said in a dazed voice. "He must have been hiding down in the cabin."

"But where'd he come from?"

Mark scratched his jaw thoughtfully. "Darned if I know. He must have climbed aboard while the boat was tied up in that cave."

"But, Mark—who?"

"If we knew that, baby, this case would probably be closed as of here and now. Thing to do is get back to *Hell's Light* and count noses. Find out who's been missing for the past few hours."

"How do we manage that trick?" I asked.

"What do you mean?"

'There's nothing on this side of Catalina. To reach White's Landing, we'd have to hike over Mt. Orizaba or search for Two Harbors' Road and try for Avalon. Either way we could never make it in our bare feet."

"How far to White's Landing?"

"About seven miles," I said. "Mt. Orizaba is over a thousand feet high. And she's rugged!"

Mark flinched. "That's out. I'm a lousy mountain climber. Besides, I've got flat feet."

"That figures. So what do we do? Build a seaweed hut, catch fish and start our own civilization?"

Mark put his arm around my shoulder and squeezed in a tender, intimate way that meant more than any words. The gesture said, I like you, Honey. When do we start with this wonderful new world?

I broke the emotional connection. "Come on, Mark. What are we going to do?"

"That's a good question," he admitted, grinning wolfishly. "Said with just the right amount of feminine naivety." His eyes drifted down to my torn bathing suit. "You might never guess it, but I'm an excellent tailor."

I smiled, "I'll be all right."

"Just happened to bring a needle and thread with me. I'd be very happy to make a stitch here and there."

"Mark," I said, "we're in a serious predicament. Now will you stop making jokes?"

"Honey, you're no joke, believe me." His eyes fell upon the blood-stained jacket and his jaw tightened. "Why don't you quit this damned business and get married?"

"But, Mark," I teased, "Fred hasn't asked me yet. And besides—"

"Fred?" the lieutenant boomed. "Why that dirty, no-good—"

The blinding glare of a searchlight cut Mark's retort into word less mouthings that literally fell apart in mid-air.

"You all right, Lieutenant Storm?" a voice boomed from behind the glare.

Mark cupped his hands around his mouth and shouted, "Who is it?"

"Chief Clements of the Avalon Police Department. What's going on?"

"We're marooned," Mark returned loudly. "Have you got an auxiliary boat you can put ashore?"

"Sure," came the reply. "I'll bring it in myself."

Mark glanced at my torn bathing suit. "Oh, and bring a blanket with you, Chief. I've got a body to wrap up."

When we were aboard the Avalon patrol boat, Mark introduced me to Chief Clements. The old, white-haired police officer had a devilish twinkle in his eyes as his mind seemed to recall the moment we met on the beach before Mark got the blanket around me.

Clements examined the blood-stained jacket after Mark told the story of our mishaps at Little Harbor.

Mark explained, "This article of clothing belonged to a man named Aces. Sam Aces. A television producer."

"From the looks of things, he's been producing all right," the chief said, poking his finger through the bullet hole.

Mark nodded. "How'd you happen to find us?"

"Important message came through from L.A. for

you. I decided to run it out to *Hell's Light* myself. They told me you'd been gone since noon, so I thought I'd scout around a bit."

"We're certainty glad you did," I said.

Clements continued. "About three miles out from Little Harbor we sighted a small boat's lights. She didn't respond to my blinker, so we let her go by."

"That was the cruiser, Chief," Mark said grimly.

"I realize that now," Clements said. "How'd the bandit get possession?"

"I figure he was stowed away somewhere during our trip around the island. As soon as we'd anchored and gone ashore, he took off."

"We'll find him," Clements assured us.

"I hope so," Mark answered. "He got away with my clothes, my revolver and a very important piece of evidence. A typewritten message Aces sent to a former associate named Caine."

Clements wiped some spray out of his eyes. "Did you say Caine? That's the man I talked to aboard *Hell's Light*. This man, Caine, said the TV people were worried about their big television star—what's his name—Swans-down!"

"Swanson," I corrected. "Bob Swanson."

"Yeah, that's the one," Clements agreed. "Caine said this Swanson disappeared about four o'clock while they were shooting a picture at White's Landing. Nobody's seen hide nor hair of him since."

Mark looked at me, gripping the edge of his upper lip in his teeth. I knew what he was thinking. I was thinking the same thing. We had arrived at Rod's cabin about six o'clock. Bob Swanson had vanished on the beach around four. During that time he could have gone to Rod's cabin and planted the note, then waited around for our arrival and stowed away aboard Chief Clements' boat.

Mark asked the Avalon police chief about the urgent message from his Los Angeles office.

"They want you back tonight," Clements said. "A new lead has turned up in the Nelson case."

"That's what I thought," Mark said, glancing at me. "We've been tracking down some of Herb's old pals. One of them, Ed Walker, was seen going into Nelson's place an hour before the murder."

The stern lights of Aces' yacht shone in the dark night. It was after midnight and I was tired and suddenly angry because Mark hadn't taken me into his confidence about this new twist in the Nelson case. I started to complain when something stopped me. Chief Clement's racy cabin cruiser was tied up at *Hell's Light*'s boat landing.

"Well, what do you know?" Mark said. "This is going to be easier than I thought. Maybe we can wind this case up tonight before I go back to L.A."

Everything aboard the *Clementine* was intact, except the typewritten note we had found in Rod's coat pocket.

Mark dressed quickly and we went aboard the yacht. Max Decker met us in the passageway outside the swimming-pool bar.

"Now see here, Lieutenant," the TV magnate roared, "I've had just about enough of your stalling tactics—"

"Where's Swanson?" Mark interrupted.

"I haven't seen him all day," Decker said. "He went to White's Landing to shoot an important scene and he hasn't returned."

Mark pushed the fat man out of the way. "I know he's somewhere on this ship. Now where is he?"

"I told you, he didn't come back—"

Rod Caine walked out on deck. Mark pounced on him. "Where's Swanson?" the lieutenant asked.

"You got me," Rod said. "Haven't seen him. Nobody has. There's a scouting party over at White's Landing now."

Mark pointed to the cruiser. "That cabin job pulled in here sometime in the last hour. Now who was at the helm?"

"I don't know," Rod said flatly. "I was in the bar. I didn't even hear the boat arrive."

People poured out of the bar. One of them was Lori Aces. Mark repeated his questions, but no one would admit having seen the cruiser tie up at the boat landing.

While Mark, Chief Clements and two Avalon policemen searched for Swanson, I changed from my torn suit and blanket into something more practical. Lori Aces followed me to my cabin. She broke down when I told her about Sam's jacket.

"I've got to tell the truth," she said. "I've really never loved Sammy. But he's such a nice guy, you got to like him. Do the police really think Sam's been murdered?"

I nodded and went back to the bar. The music, laughter and whiskey were still flowing. It made me sick. Sam Aces might be dead but nobody seemed to care.

I glanced at Joe Meeler, the writer who had replaced Rod Caine on the Swanson show. He was slumped forward on the bar, apparently sleeping off his good time. That seemed funny. I didn't think little Joe drank.

I waded over to rouse him. He couldn't be roused.

Joe was dead, a butcher knife stuck between his ribs.

After examining the weapon, Mark questioned the drunken patrons at the swimming-pool bar. "How long's he been sitting here, anyone know?"

"Not long," one of the cameramen answered. "I'd guess a half hour. Maybe less."

"Did he come in alone?"

No answer.

"Was Swanson in the bar during the past half hour?"

Still no answer.

"What the hell do you people do?" Mark burst. "Pour this stuff on your eyeballs?"

A few inarticulate grunts.

"Did Swanson dislike Meeler?" the lieutenant continued.

"He was always shouting at him," another cameraman said.

A little red-haired starlet added, "So what? Bob Swanson shouts at everyone on the set."

"Did they ever argue?" Mark demanded.

Ann Claypool said, "They did today. It was pretty

violent. I thought Bob was going to chop Joe into little pieces."

"What was the argument about?" Mark asked.

"A sailboat scene," Ann continued. "According to the script. Bob was supposed to follow me down the ladder into the sailboat. But he wanted to reverse the procedure. I was wearing a full circle skirt—"

"I get the idea," Mark said. "What happened?"

"Joe called Swanson a twisted lecherous bastard and the sparks flew."

"Did Swanson fire Meeler?"

"No," Ann said. "Bob just went haywire, shouting and raving. That's when he disappeared. We couldn't find him after that."

Mark looked at me and his mouth tightened. I knew what he was thinking. How could Golden Boy have entered and left the swimming-pool area without being seen by one of his television compatriots—much less silently commit a murder which involved something as unwieldy as a butcher knife. Meeler must have been completely unaware that he was about to die. If he'd had any kind of warning, the TV writer surely would have alerted others in the bar.

After Meeler's body was loaded aboard the Avalon patrol boat, I walked down to the float with Mark and Chief Clements.

"The Coast Guard will probably send out an investigating party," Mark explained. "I got a blood-sample scraping from the chest and will try to match it with the stains on the jacket. I'll be back tomorrow, after I check out this character, Walker, who turned up in the Nelson case. Meanwhile, stay out of mischief, understand?"

"That's a pretty tall order, Lieutenant, but I'll try. Incidentally, why did you fail to tell me about this guy Walker?"

Mark ignored the question, climbed into the patrol boat, then turned and took my hand. "I understand Decker skipped out on a water taxi while we were searching for Swanson. He isn't out of this by any means. I want him back on this ship by tomorrow. If the Avalon police can't find him, it's up to you, Honey. There are some places a dame can get into that even a cop can't."

I nodded, kissed his cheek and thanked him for our exciting sojourn to Little Harbor.

"We'll have to do it again sometime," Mark smiled. "Under different circumstances."

The patrol boat rocked, kicked up a dark crest that washed over the float and moved away into the night.

"Don't forget the prints on that knife!" I yelled.

"I won't!" Mark called back. "And don't you forget to keep yourself out of trouble!"

I walked up to the main deck, meeting Rod Caine at the top of the steps. He was strangely apologetic about Meeler's death.

"I can't understand how it could have happened," he said dejectedly. "Joe was a damned good writer. He was doing a better job on the show than I ever did. I'm really sorry about this, believe me."

"Did Lori tell you about Aces' jacket?"

"Yeah."

'Were you surprised?"

"Hell, yes, I was surprised," Rod said. "I still can't believe he's dead, though."

We walked to the bow of the ship. Rod lit two cigarettes and handed me one. I thought of Aces' habit of doing the same thing.

"Did Aces ever send you a note inviting you aboard this ship?" I asked.

"Many times," Rod said quietly. "I've spent some wonderful days aboard *Hell's Light*."

"I mean recently."

"Of course not. I told you I didn't see or hear from Sam from the time I ran out of Lori's bedroom until last night."

"You're absolutely certain?"

Rod cocked his head suspiciously. "Now what does that mean?"

I flipped my cigarette overboard. "We found a note in your coat pocket."

"When?"

"Early this evening in your cabin. One thing we didn't find was your lab equipment."

Rod shook his head dazedly. "You were in my cabin early this evening?"

"That's right."

"And you didn't find my equipment? Did you look in the metal case on the kitchen table?"

"We didn't find a thing. Not even the metal case."

"But I left it on the table in the kitchen. Lori'll tell you. She watched me make the tests.

"We found Sam's glass and that's all."

Rod appeared genuinely dumbfounded. If this was an act, it was a good one. But then, I was surrounded by a ship full of actors, so his performance didn't convince me entirely.

"Believe me," Rod said, "that equipment was on the table when Lori and I left. Someone must have taken it while we were gone."

"Who steals that sort of thing?"

"I don't know."

"What about the note?"

"I can't explain that," Rod said. "If there was a note in my pocket, someone planted it there."

"Let's lay a few things on the line," I said. "What was Swanson talking about last night when he said you'd know why he got mad in the bar?"

Rod didn't answer for a long time. He pinched out his cigarette and tossed it into the water. "You want it straight?"

"Straight as you can make it."

"All right. I guess there's nothing to lose now. Swanson found out I was living on Catalina. I don't know how he found out, but he did. He came to see me about three weeks ago. Said his visit had to be strictly confidential. He told me if it didn't remain secret, if his personal dealings with me ever came out in the open, he'd kill me dead in the writing field."

"What was he after?"

Rod wiped his hands across his forehead. "A personal contract for my services on the Swanson show."

"I don't understand."

"I didn't understand at first myself. Then he explained that he and Decker were planning to force Aces out as producer. They had some kind of gimmick. I don't know what it was, but he wanted me back as writer. I told him I didn't want the deal, that I was happy with what I was doing. Then he really got tough. Promised me nothing but trouble if I didn't sign the contract. So I signed. What else could I do?"

"Now we're getting somewhere," I said. "You met him that night in the Golden Slipper, not accidentally, but on purpose."

"That's right. He told me to be there after the show because he wanted to iron out a few last details."

"And what were these details?"

"I don't know," Rod said vaguely. "He was crocked when I got there. Loaded to the gills. I told you how he kidded me about the drink he was taking to Aces."

I nodded.

"Decker was there, too. I tried to get something concrete out of him, but he was flying three ways to the moon himself and I got nothing—except an ultimatum from Swanson to show up in his office on the twenty-fifth."

"You mean last Monday? The day I signed my contract?"

"Yeah. I know I told you I hadn't been back to town since that time in the Golden Slipper, but I had to lie. Don't you understand? Swanson had me. I figured if I told you everything, it would get back to him. My writing career would have been but the window. I couldn't take the chance."

"Okay. I understand. What happened last Monday?"

"Swanson told me Aces would be out inside of two weeks. That meant Meeler, too. I argued. Told him Joe Meeler was doing a damn good job and ought to be retained. I said the same thing about Aces, and Swanson nearly hit the ceiling. He said if he could, he'd send Sam Aces right to the scrap heap."

"Then Swanson thought you were pulling a fast one when he saw you last night with Aces."

"Sure," Rod said. "He probably thought I was breaking his confidence and making a separate deal with Sam. Certainly he never expected to walk in that bar and see the two of us talking together."

I searched for holes in his story. There was only one opening I could find. "How come none of your old cronies recognized you in the Golden Slipper, or last Monday at Television Riviera?"

"It took a while for the plastic surgery to heal. During that time I couldn't shave so I grew a pretty heavy beard. Swanson didn't even recognize me the day he came over from the mainland. I shaved for the first time the afternoon I found you wading around in my abalone beds."

He flashed that infectious smile. I liked this guy. I couldn't help it.

"Mister," I whispered, "I'm very glad we met."

"So am I. I saw you Monday at the studio and you know what I said to myself? There's the most beautiful woman alive. Why don't you ask her to marry you, buy a hunk of your crazy island and never come back to civilization again?"

"Why didn't you?" I teased.

"Because," he said, "I knew there'd be ten thousand guys ahead of me in line."

"What if I told you there weren't ten thousand guys?"

"I'd say you're the biggest liar in the world." He took my face in his hands and kissed me.

He looked at me tenderly, "You know, I started something the night we met that I never got a chance to finish."

A crazy hot feeling boiled up in my stomach. Before I could make a move, Rod picked me up, carried me to my cabin and locked the door.

The horn of a big ship passing outside tore the darkness with its sound. He unbuttoned my sweater and slipped it gently off my shoulders.

Suddenly there was another sound. Loud footsteps running hurriedly on the deck. It was a sound filled with urgency—with deadliness.

Rod whirled toward the doorway, snapped open the lock and stepped outside. He disappeared as the night wind pushed the door closed. I waited tensely as Rod's footsteps faded in the distance. New rain pattered on the windows. When I peeked through one of the curtains, a yellowish face rose up, stared at me and disappeared.

Then there was knock at the door. For an instant I

was frightened. Really frightened. A killer was loose aboard *Hell's Light*. I forced back my female instincts, assumed my role of private detective, and answered.

"'Who is it?" I asked.

"Carruthers, ma'am."

"Who?"

"Carruthers. One of the ship's crew, ma'am. I found something I think you and your police friend ought to see."

"Just a minute." I switched on the table lamp and crossed to my closet for a negligee.

Carruthers, his weather-beaten face damp with rain, stood outside the door. He was wearing a yellow hat and slicker and looked like something hauled straight out of the Sargasso Sea. But what really shook me was the instrument he held.

It was a knife. A butcher knife. Exactly like the one Mark had pulled from the dead body of Joe Meeler.

ELEVEN

CARRUTHERS SHOVED THE KNIFE TOWARD ME. "FOUND it down on B Deck near one of the lifeboats," he said. "Looks like a trick gadget of some kind."

"What do you mean?" I asked.

"Here, I'll show you, ma'am." He took the butcher knife in his right hand, swung it back and rammed it squarely in his chest.

He should have been ready for a pine box or leaking so much plasma the blood bank could have closed down for a week. But he wasn't even scratched.

The old man smiled. "Amazing, ain't it?"

"Let me see that again." I examined the knife. It was apparently spring-loaded, allowing the blade to collapse on contact into a narrow slit in the handle.

Carruthers chuckled, remarked about weird inventions and vanished into the night. A short time later Rod appeared, breathless and wet from the rain.

"I don't get it," he said. "There was somebody out

there, but he vanished before I could catch up with him."

I showed Rod the trick knife and gave Carruthers' account of the discovery on B Deck. "What do you make of the gadget?" I asked.

"It's what they call a breakaway. Must be a Swanson TV prop." Rod examined the instrument. "Wonder how it got down there. I understood from Lud Norman that all props are kept on main deck in back of the swimming pool."

"Looks exactly like the one we found in Meeler," I said.

"Yeah, but that was no breakaway."

I pointed to the handle. "Did you notice this brown stain?"

"Makeup," Rod nodded. "TV people just don't know when to stop with the stuff. Ann Claypool's one of the worst. She spreads it on every part of her that shows."

"Speaking of Ann Claypool, what gives between you two?"

"What do you mean?" Rod demanded. "I—I'm an old friend. Vince Claypool and I went to college together."

"Vince was her husband?"

"Yeah. A nice guy. We opened up a sporting-goods shop together after graduation. That's when Vince met Ann. I never liked her—must have told him a thousand times she was no good. But he married her anyway."

"Was Ann really crazy about him?"

"Are you kidding? She's crazy about only two things—Ann Claypool and sex. She's one of those physical combinations that spells dynamite. Little woman, big bust. She's always out to prove something. Little people usually are. I imagine you can guess what she's trying to prove."

"You don't think she was sorry to see her husband die?"

"Hell, no! Vince had a ten-thousand dollar G.I. term policy. She's been having a ball on that poor bastard. If he only knew."

"But Ann gave me the impression she hated Aces' guts for sending Vince Claypool out on that underwater assignment."

"Sounds like Ann all right. Always with the sad story when she's in the chips and living high. The time to be careful of Annie is when she acts deliriously, sexapatingly happy like she did last night."

"Do you think she and Swanson could be in this together?"

"Who knows?" Rod shrugged his shoulders. "What would Ann get out of it?"

"The female lead in the Swanson show."

A stunned look sprang onto Rod's face. "Hell! I'd forgotten about Decker replacing you with Claypool!"

"It was apparently a joint decision introduced by Swanson and approved by Decker," I added.

"And meted out the morning after Aces disappeared." Rod rubbed his hands together vigorously. "I think you've got something, Honey. Something big."

"Think back," I suggested. "It would have been pretty tough for Swanson to poison Aces' drink. He was around only a few seconds. But with Annie it was different. A lot different."

"You can say that again," Rod agreed. "She was all over the bar. It wouldn't have been easy, but nothing's too tough for little Annie if there's money in the deal."

I picked up the breakaway knife again. "But why murder Joe Meeler? Do you suppose he saw Ann or Golden Boy slip something in Aces' drink?"

"Could be!"

"Maybe Meeler was mixed up in the plot himself."

Rod shook his head. "Not Joe Meeler. He wouldn't hurt a gnat if he could help it."

"Joe never drank, did he?"

"Used to," Rod said. "Plenty. He cut off the alcohol after his operation."

"What was his trouble?"

"Peptic ulcers. Bad. Damn near killed him."

"If that's the case, why was he always hanging around the bar?"

Rod said, "Habit, I guess. In the old days he always did his best writing in bars. Liked the atmosphere."

"Seems almost prophetic he had to die in one."

"Yeah."

"What time is it?" I asked.

"Little after three. Why are you always so interested in the time?"

I stepped into the bathroom, slipped out of my negligee and into a swimsuit. "If the swimming-pool area is cleared out, I'd like to try to reenact Meeler's murder. Are you game?"

Rod's forehead ridged slightly. "I don't know. What do you want me to do?"

"Play the murderer."

"Will you cut it out?" he said angrily.

"All right, I'll play the murderer if it makes you any happier."

Just as long as you don't substitute that breakaway knife for the real thing."

I whirled around and grabbed Rod. "That's it!" I exclaimed. "That's how it was done!"

"What do you mean?"

"Somebody who knew Meeler could have substituted a real knife for the phony while they were discussing a scene."

I tossed a sweater over my shoulders and took his arm. "Come on, I'll show you."

The bar and swimming pool were dark. I switched on some lights and led Rod through the water to the exact stool where Meeler was found.

"You sit here," I said.

He followed my instructions resignedly. "Okay, now what?"

I waded back to the edge of the pool. "Now, I'm Swanson. You're Meeler. The bar is filled with people having a wild time."

"Yeah," Rod said. "Only if you're Swanson and these characters have been looking for you all day, don't you think you'd better come in with a tent over your head? Nothing would be more obvious than Golden Boy's chubby jowls and thick arms."

That made sense. Swanson couldn't have walked in unnoticed. He'd have attracted as much attention as a man wearing kilts and playing a bagpipe in the ladies' lounge of the Statler Hotel.

"Check," I said, circling around the edge of the pool. At the deep end, I stopped to survey the bar. "How about an approach from this direction? He could dive in and swim underwater. Swanson's a crackerjack at that sort of thing."

Rod pointed out a very important factor. There was no way into the pool area from the deep end. Swanson still would have had to pass through the game zone on the shallow side in order to reach the nine-foot depth.

I took off my sweater and plunged into the water. In the middle of the deep end wall I noticed a small porthole. Through the thick glass I could see a narrow passageway on B Deck. Then I saw something else. There was a lifeboat suspended along the side of the corridor. I surfaced.

"Rod!"

He almost fell off his stool. "'What's the matter? You find another body?"

"No!" I yelled, swimming quickly to the bar. "I think I've got the answer to how the murderer entered and left unnoticed."

"Don't tell me he was in the pool all the time using a snorkel and pretending to be the Creature from the Black Lagoon!"

"Don't be smart!" I climbed over the top of the circular bar to the inside where the glasses and liquor were stored. The floor, about two-feet wide and made of steel plating, was dry and raised well above the level of the pool bottom. Obviously a circular area the size of the bar was built underneath. I searched for a trap door.

About three feet from Rod's stool I found one. The door raised easily. I climbed down a ladder into a store-room that was dark and foreboding with its stacked cases of whiskey. Rod's face appeared in the trap door opening.

"What's down there?" he asked.

"Enough giggle juice to float a battleship. Take a look for yourself."

Rod accepted my invitation. He was overwhelmed by the quantity of liquor in the storeroom.

"Courtesy of Grandpa Aces," I said. "No doubt Sam got around certain provisions of the will by listing this as necessary ship's stores."

"Holy smokes," Rod exclaimed, "I didn't know this room was down here. Sam always carried enough stock on the shelves around the bar to last any trip we ever made to Catalina and back. This looks like enough for a three-year cruise around the world."

"That's for sure," I agreed. "Let's see how they got this stuff in here. They couldn't have brought all these cases through the swimming pool."

I was right. A watertight door led us out onto B Deck only a few yards from the lifeboat. I'd seen through the underwater porthole in the pool. Carruthers said he'd found the trick knife on B Deck near a lifeboat. I was willing to bet this was where he'd made his discovery.

"Okay," Rod said, "how'd Swanson do it? And, more important, why?"

"Meeler saw the *Clementine* arrive," I explained. "He recognized the man at the wheel. He probably exchanged friendly greetings with the killer not realizing he was signing his own death certificate. They retired to the bar where Meeler was shown the breakaway knife. Then, in the confusion of my arrival with Chief Clements, while everyone poured out on deck, the killer plunged the real blade into Meeler and escaped through the opening in the bar floor."

"Sounds reasonable up to a point," Rod said. "But you still haven't explained Bob Swanson's presence in the bar and why someone besides Meeler didn't recognize him."

I answered quickly, "He must have put on some sort of disguise before joining Meeler. This would explain the makeup smudges on the breakaway handle."

"Fantastic, Honey. Then you really believe Swanson's the killer?"

"I don't know."

"But, you just said—"

"Forget what I said, Rod. I don't know what's wrong here, but something's haywire."

"I don't get you."

"Herb Nelson was bludgeoned to death. Sam Aces was apparently poisoned and then shot at close range. Joe Meeler—stabbed. All three murders about as brutal as possible. I'm convinced they were committed by one and the same person. But who? Swanson's almost too obvious. Decker had arsenic in his possession. You said you were going to test for arsenic and yet we couldn't find any of your equipment. We did find a highly suspicious note which led to Aces' bloodstained jacket."

Rod Caine reddened. "Now, listen, once and for all, I'm not the killer!"

"If you're not," I said, "the real villain in this piece is trying mighty hard to make you look guilty. Believe me, Rod, you'd be behind bars right now if Chief Clements hadn't verified your presence aboard *Hell's Light* while Mark and I were searching for Aces. The murderer probably hoped you'd leave the yacht and go home so that you d be the logical stowaway suspect."

Rod glanced away for an instant. Then he said, "I was on the float ready to go back to my place when Chief Clements pulled up in the police boat."

"Now you're talking the killer's language."

"But that's the strange part," Rod said uneasily. "I didn't plan to go home at all until Ann Claypool told me Swanson faked his disappearance in order to meet me at my cabin."

I recoiled, "You're joking!"

"No. She said he wanted to talk more about the show. I asked her how long he'd been waiting and she guessed about two hours. I really blew my top when I heard that."

"Did you go to your cabin then?"

"Of course. But Swanson wasn't there, so I waited around thinking he'd come back."

"How long did you wait?" I demanded.

"All evening. I got back to *Hell's Light* a short time before you did."

"And you mean to tell me you never noticed your lab equipment was gone from the kitchen table?"

"No—no, I didn't," Rod stammered. "I don't think I even went into the kitchen. That's why I was so surprised when you said the portable case was gone."

I felt like tearing my hair out by the roots. Why hadn't I thought to ask someone if Rod had been missing during the evening. Clements had talked to him aboard the yacht, but neither Mark nor I had bothered to ask what time that discussion occurred. Could it have been early enough for Rod Caine to swim unseen to the boat cave and steal aboard the *Clementine*?

"I know it sound suspicious, Honey, but—"

"Why didn't you tell me this before?" I demanded, suddenly on the defensive again.

"Because I figured Ann Claypool and Swanson decoyed me to the cabin to try and hook Aces' murder onto me. But it didn't add up somehow. I wanted to talk to Ann before I spilled the story to you."

I climbed over the bar into the pool. "All right. Let's visit Miss Claypool and get her version of the story."

"You don't expect her to admit anything if she's mixed up in this, do you?"

"I don't know what to expect," I said angrily. "Do you want to come along while I ask her?"

Rod vaulted over the rail into the water. "You're damn right! I'm getting tired of being the fall guy around here!"

We went to Ann's cabin. There were no lights. I knocked gently. No answer. Rod banged. Still no answer. He tried the knob and it turned. We entered and switched on the light. The bed was turned back, but Ann wasn't in it.

"She's gone," Rod said. "Skipped. Does that answer your questions?"

"No!" I opened the closet. Her clothes were still there. Then I heard Rod's voice from the bathroom. It sounded twisted, as if someone had gripped him about the throat.

"She's in here," he said.

I entered the bathroom where Rod was bent awkwardly over a pink tub. In the water, Ann Claypool floated face up, stark naked, long black hair curled around her face like thick strands of seaweed. Her bright green eyes were wide and watery and she stared up at us for a long moment before Rod straightened up.

"She—she's dead," he managed. "What in hell could have happened?"

I leaned over the tub. Two livid thumb prints were on her white neck. There was no point in answering Rod's question. It was too obvious.

TWELVE

STRANGULATILON IS A BRUTAL WAY TO DIE, BUT IN death Ann Claypool seemed quietly and beautifully resigned to her fate.

Her bathroom was a dismal wreck. The medicine cabinet was half torn from its hinges. A cocktail glass was shattered on the floor. Broken fragments lay glittering in tiny pools of water that had spilled over the side of the tub as she apparently had struggled with her killer. An ashtray and several lipstick-stained cigarette butts floated around the lifeless nude body.

Rod Caine stood beside the tub, arms limp at his sides, eyes riveted on Ann. "I don't understand," he murmured. "This isn't possible."

"Why not?" I asked quickly.

"Well—I don't know," Rod stammered. "This just doesn't make sense. Who—who'd want to kill Ann?"

"Maybe somebody had to."

"What do you mean?"

We walked out onto the deck. The black sea was growing amber with the coming dawn. I looked at his unshaven face. "Maybe she was about to reveal the killer's identity."

"Honey, quit looking at me like that! I didn't do it. How could I? I've been with you all night."

"I'm not blaming you," Rod, I said, shaking my head. "I'm blaming myself for being so dumb. For not sticking to my guns."

"About what?"

"About a certain theory I had concerning Sam Aces." I glanced toward Ann's stateroom. "Listen, Rod, after the police arrive I'm going into Avalon. For the next twenty-four hours you must not leave this yacht for any reason. Do you understand?"

"No, I don't. Why can't I go with you?"

"Because I've got a hunch," I said. "A real big hunch that somebody else is going to die and the killer will want you in the vicinity when it happens."

"You mean Avalon?"

"That's right. You've got to be able to prove you were aboard this yacht. I don't care whether you get a death warning, a secret message or a vision—don't leave this ship!"

Rod grinned. "Honey, what's going on? What'd you find in there? A death image in Ann's eyes? An important clue? What?"

"I'll let you know when I get back from Avalon. Maybe I'm crazy. But, believe me, I'm going to find out."

Glittering spray danced in the brilliant morning light as the patrol boat sliced through the waters outside Avalon Bay. Chief Clements sat beside me, his wrinkled mouth closed in stony silence. He'd been that way ever since in the bathroom, when he looked into Ann Claypool's wet staring eyes. Three murders in one night had been too much for the old police officer.

I chipped through his marbelized exterior with a question about Decker.

"We haven't been able to find him," Clements admitted wearily. "After dropping Lieutenant Storm at the airport last night, we searched Decker's yacht. We found absolutely nothing."

"How's Avalon as a hideout?"

The chief scowled. "Best this side of the French Riviera. You know the setup. Hundreds of cabins in the Villa, homes on the hill, homes in the canyon, all sorts of ocean caves, two piers, the casino—it's endless. If Decker's on the island, it might take us a month to blast him out."

"And if he's aboard another yacht?"

"Then it's hardly possible unless we get a strong lead. Yesterday there were almost three hundred boats anchored in Avalon Bay."

The red-tiled roof of the huge casino building appeared out of the swirling spray. Over the roar of the police-boat engines could be heard the hillside chimes, pealing from the white tower above the bay.

I asked the chief if any efforts were being made to retrieve Sam Aces' body.

"Two divers have been down exploring the reefs at Little Harbor since dawn," Clements said. "Frankly, I doubt if we'll ever find the body."

Our boat swept past a fabulous triple-masted schooner. The police officer pointed at the words, *Decker's Dilemma*, painted on the side of the huge sailing vessel. Obviously, the ship belonged to Man Mountain Max. That gave the two of us something in common. A dilemma. It was my job to find a *dead* man before he committed another murder.

I phoned Mark from the Avalon police station. He hadn't slept all night and admitted he was up to his ears with the Nelson case. "We still haven't located this suspect, Walker," the lieutenant said. "He seems to have vanished into thin air."

Mark was jolted when I told him about Ann Claypool. "Holy smokes!" he roared. "We're dealing with a maniac!"

"A clever maniac," I said.

"We've got an APB out on Swanson," Mark told me. "The same goes for Decker. But it sounds to me like they're still in your vicinity. Has Clements found Aces' body yet?"

"No. And he's not going to."

"What do you mean?"

"I don't believe Sam Aces is dead."

"Here we go again!" Mark cried. "Where do you get these ideas?"

"It all fits a pattern, Lieutenant," I said angrily. "Do you want to hear it?"

"Go ahead."

"Aces murdered Herb Nelson."

"Why?" Mark demanded.

"I don't know yet," I said hesitantly, "but when I find him I'll know the answer to that question."

Mark Storm groaned wearily. "Before you waste any more of the taxpayers' money on this telephone call, let me tell you something.

"What?"

"Remember the blood-sample scrapings I took from the trunk?"

"Of course I remember. They don't match with the stains on the jacket, do they?"

Mark swiftly squashed my theory. "They match perfectly. In fact, from corresponding medical samples we've proved conclusively the blood stains in both cases belonged to Sam Aces. You want to know something else?"

"Go ahead."

"You won't believe this, Honey, but Herb Nelson wasn't the little white god we all thought he was. For the past few years he's been pushing heroin."

"You're lying!"

"I wish I were," Mark said. "This morning we picked up a couple of jokers in the vicinity of Nelson's apartment. They had needle marks clear up to their armpits. They admitted Herb's been selling junk to them and dozens of other punks for years."

"Can they prove it?" I demanded.

"They don't have to. We went up to the apartment,

ripped open a few suspicious wall boards and discovered a hiding place. There were a number of needles, old spoons and H caps. So we made another autopsy on his body about a half hour ago. He'd been using the stuff himself."

"Oh, no!" I felt for a chair and slumped down.

"Then a few minutes ago," Mark continued, "I got a call from the San Diego police. They've just made a big roundup of Southern California heroin suppliers at the border. One of them had a junk list."

"What's that?"

"Names of pushers in various areas and who kept them supplied. Herb Nelson's name was on that list."

"Who was his supplier?"

"A man named Sam Aces."

For a long moment I couldn't get my breath, then I said, "It—it couldn't be the same one."

"We don't know for sure," Mark said. "There may be another Sam Aces, but I doubt it. Too many strong links; the old friend routine; Sam trying to get Herb a spot on the Swanson show. It all adds up. Honey, I'm afraid your two clients were a couple of bad boys.

"Mark," I protested, "I can believe it of Sam Aces, he was no archangel—but, Herb Nelson—"

"Yeah, I know what you mean. I felt sick when they brought in that stuff from his apartment. I didn't believe it until I got that phone call from San Diego."

"So where does that leave us?" I asked after a moment. "Well, this suspect, Walker, is a known user. It's my guess he went to Herb's apartment, demanded some junk, didn't have the money and was forced to kill him to get what he wanted. Where we go from there, I don't know. My theory is that Bob Swanson murdered Aces and then killed Meeler to conceal the crime. He added Ann Claypool to the list when she threatened to reveal her part in the plan."

I glanced up as Chief Clements came into his office. "Listen, Mark, the Avalon lab is making a set of prints from the thumb impressions found on Ann Claypool's neck. The chief says he'll have them flown to the mainland as soon as they're ready. I imagine they'll do a lot toward straightening us out, once and for all."

Mark said, "I hope so."

"When will you be able to get here?"

"Tonight," Mark said, "at the earliest. But I'll call Clements just as soon as we've matched those prints."

"Okay. Hey, I almost forgot! How about fingerprints on that butcher knife?"

"Plenty of them," the lieutenant answered. "All belonging to Mr. Joseph Meeler."

"Great," I said. "Now all we have to do is find out the thumb marks on Ann Claypool's throat are her own and that Sam Aces shot himself."

Mark growled, "Rotten business, isn't it? Well, are you about ready to settle down and get married?"

"Who thinks about marriage when they're having a ball at Catalina?"

Mark missed the humor, swore loudly and said, "Have it your own way, you voluptuous blonde bird-dog. But one of these days you're going to get yourself into a hole six-feet deep and then nobody's going to be able to dig you out except a guy with a shovel."

"Remind me to call for Perry Mason."

He finally softened, warned me to keep on the alert for both Decker and Swanson and ended the conversation.

I walked to the island villas and rented one of the small cabins. The day was hot and the air acrid as if someone had shipped in a slice of Los Angeles smog.

I freshened my lipstick, slipped into a cool dress and walked outside along the front cabins. That was a mistake! One of the doors suddenly flew open and a large hand pulled me inside the room.

Before I could get my bearings I was flat on my back and a big kid with thick reddish hair was trying to get my dress up. I put my heel in the middle of his stomach and he reeled across the room, landing on a small table.

The piece of furniture collapsed, pitching the startled young man to the floor. He got up slowly. I thought about reaching for my .32 but vetoed the idea in favor of some juvenile rehabilitation. The kid couldn't have been more than nineteen.

"What's your problem?" I asked, dusting myself off. "You the island doctor, or was the physical examination just for kicks?"

"I thought you were somebody else," he said, shaking his head. "I been expecting a girl named Toni. You look just like her."

"Toni must be quite a gal," I said.

He had a bad complexion and thick eyebrows. He

said, "Don't get me wrong. I didn't want to hurt you. It was all a mistake."

"Look," I said carefully. "Let's level a little, what do you say? You saw me through the window, liked what you saw and decided to have some. Isn't that about it?"

He ran his fingers nervously through his hair. "Well— I—I wasn't going to hurt you."

As I turned for the door, a rusted tin box caught my eye. It was surrounded by a collection of bright shells.

"Where'd you get that?" I demanded.

"What?"

"That metal case."

He looked frightened. "I dunno. I picked it up somewhere. Why?"

"Where'd you pick it up?"

"In the water. It—was at the bottom in a nest of sea anemone."

"Where?" I asked. "White's Landing? Little Harbor? You don't pick up articles like this every day. Where'd you find it?"

He made half gestures. "In the bay. Late yesterday afternoon. I'm an undersea diver. I work with the glass-bottom boats. Is something wrong?"

The initials RC were engraved in the top of the case. I opened the lid. No mistake. Rod had told the truth about owning lab equipment, but how in Hades had this case wound up at the bottom of Avalon Bay?

"Look," I said to the kid, "a friend of mine lost this, and it's important that I find out where."

The kid seemed confused.

"Could you locate the spot again if you had to?"

"I—I guess so," he said.

"Will you take me there?"

"Well—sure," he stammered. "When do you want to go?"

"As soon as I can change into a swimsuit. Is that okay with you?"

I returned a few minutes later. He glanced at the V-slashed neckline of my tiger-striped suit, swallowed hard and introduced himself. "Name's Marble. Danny Marble. I bunk with a couple of guys from my home town. They went over to the mainland yesterday. I guess I've been lonesome. That's why I wanted to talk to you—"

"No explanation needed," I said. "Come on, Danny. Let's go for a boat ride."

We walked to the Pleasure Pier where Danny borrowed a small five-horse putter from a friend, and we headed out into the bay. The sun was blistering hot.

Danny cut the engine about a hundred yards off from the red-roofed Casino. "This is the spot," he said decisively. "I did a special dive here yesterday because there's a lot of Iodine Kelp for the people to see."

"What's that?"

"Iodine Kelp is the ocean's tallest plant." Danny handed me a face mask with an extra-large window. "Here! Stick your head over the side and take a look for yourself."

I fastened the mask over my eyes and followed his instructions. The bottom was about twenty feet below the surface and very sandy. Giant ribbons of green kelp twisted up from the ocean floor and, like weird ballet dancers, seemed to sway in a soundless, fantastic rhythm. It was beautiful, but I was more interested in the treasure that Dan had brought up from the deep.

I flipped off the mask and studied the surrounding area. Twenty yards away lay the three-masted schooner, *Decker's Dilemma*.

"Danny, do you know that ship?" I pointed at the large sea craft.

"Sure. She's been around for several days. A big television man owns her."

"Has she moved at all to your knowledge?"

"I don't think so," Danny said. "She's secured bow and stern."

I held up the metal case. "How much would you guess this thing weighs?"

"About ten pounds, maybe less."

"How far could you throw it if you wanted to?"

"I dunno," Danny said, scratching his head. He examined the case. "You can grip it pretty easy by this metal handle." He surveyed the waters around the putter. "I guess I could heave it about as far as that schooner."

I nodded. "That was about my guess, too. Let's go over there."

"Where?"

"The schooner. I want to go aboard."

Danny groaned. "Are you crazy? You can't go aboard

a ship just because you've got an urge to do it. Especially that one."

"Why?"

"Rough crew," Danny said. "Real rough. I think this television guy keeps 'em around for protection."

"How do you know they're rough?"

The youth shook his head. "Couple of the boys and I got—drunk the other night during the storm. We went for a boat ride and swamped near the schooner. We barely managed to climb aboard when these three big goons jumped us. And I really mean jumped! We put up a whale of a battle, but they had us on size, weight, experience, everything."

"What finally happened?"

"What do you think? We got tossed in the drink. It was just lucky none of us drowned."

I scanned the quiet decks of the schooner. "Nice guys! I'd like to meet them."

"You're kidding!"

"Cross my heart. Want me to drop you somewhere first?"

The big kid swallowed hard. "I'll stick. I might get killed doing it, but I'll play along."

I patted his cheek. "That's my boy! Let's go!"

Danny fired up the engine and we cleaved the short distance to Decker's schooner. Nobody appeared. He tied the boat to the landing ladder and we started up the steps.

"I hope you know what you're doing," he said. "I've got to work this afternoon and I don't want to do it in splints."

I didn't answer. My thoughts were concentrating on Decker's disappearance and the discovery of Rod's metal case near the TV king's yacht. Someone had stolen the lab equipment and apparently brought it back to Decker's schooner. But why? Bob Swanson and Max Decker were around somewhere and I had a feeling I was getting closer by the second.

The three bodyguards suddenly popped up out of a hatch. They had more muscle than a herd of bulls. I was hoping, in contrast, they had less brains than a pack of fleas.

"Hey, you two!" the ugliest yelled. "Get off this ship before we throw you off."

"I'll bet you three gentlemen combined couldn't throw an oyster into a pot of stew," I answered.

They rose up out of the hatch with Herculean precision. They must have weighed two hundred pounds each.

"Lady," the second ugliest boomed, "I could personally toss you over the Casino with my little finger!"

I laughed. "I'll bet your little finger is so muscle-bound you can't raise it high enough to scratch your own elbow."

Danny was shaking all the way down to his toes. "What are you trying to do?" he whispered.

I smiled at him. "Don't worry!" Then I said to the three bodyguards, "If you're so tough why don't you take us on one at a time?"

They grunted. The ugliest came on, wrapped his hairy arms around my waist and squeezed. I got a leg up under him and ripped hard with my knee. He grabbed his stomach, bent over and I drop-kicked him neatly over the side. He made one tremendous splash and disappeared.

THIRTEEN

THE SECOND MUSCLE MAN ADVANCED ANGRILY AND reached for me. I caught him by the wrist, snapped his arm over my shoulder and leaned into the wind. When he hit high C, I flipped him in a circular arc. He hit the water head first.

The third pug, refusing to believe his eyes, got off to a bad start even before he moved out of the starting gate. He made some King Kong noises, flexing and snorting as if he were working up to an appearance before the crowds. Then he was off and running. But he hit a newly waxed section of deck. The next time I looked, he was stretched completely out, pawing at the sky as he catapulted into the water, pancaking with a sickening swoosh.

By the time the three of them had surfaced, a thin, white-haired man in an expensive-looking robe came out on deck, swearing and waving violently at them.

"You bums," he yelled. "You pasty-faced, weak-kneed rascals! You couldn't lick an old lady with her hands tied behind her back. You're fired!"

He aimed a shotgun at the bobbing figures. "Swim for shore before I put a pound of buckshot in your yellow-bellied drawers!"

They headed for the beach, ripping the water open with their powerful arms. Danny Marble heaved a big sigh of relief. I approached the skinny little man with the shotgun.

"Thanks," I said.

"Don't thank me," he said angrily. "When I see more than six hundred pounds of beef being tossed around by a woman, I know it's time Max Decker got some new hands aboard this yacht."

He introduced himself as Philip Hickman, president of the Radio-Television Corporation. "We own a sizeable interest in Decker's WES network."

"I'm looking for Decker," I said.

"Everyone is," Hickman returned. "You a female cop?"

"Private investigator. Sam Aces was my client until he disappeared. I suppose you've heard about the blood-stained jacket?"

Hickman winced. "Yes, the police told me last night. I liked Aces. He had a lot of executive ability. Too bad this had to happen right now."

"What do you mean?"

"During our meeting," Hickman explained. "Four of us flew all the way from New York for this get-together. Unfortunately, Aces never learned of our decision."

"I don't follow you."

"Well," Hickman continued. "Decker owns the largest block of stock in World Broadcasting System, but a board of directors actually runs the network. None of the board, including myself, have been too happy with Max's operation of the Western net at Television Riviera. This has been going on for more than a year. He's incompetent when it comes to mixing with people and personalities. So the board voted to move Decker back to WBS headquarters in New York and replace him in Hollywood with Sam Aces."

I caught my breath.

Hickman continued. "We had only one obstacle, that was Decker. He'd always been jealous of Aces for some reason. But Max finally gave in last Monday morning and agreed to turn his desk over to Sam."

"Why didn't someone tell Aces?" I demanded. "That was one of Decker's stipulations. Aces wasn't to be notified until after the Catalina trip." Hickman shook his head. "I don't know exactly why. Max is a strange man."

"You can say that again. Did you know Decker had been secretly planning to oust Aces?"

"No, I knew nothing about such a thing."

"Did you know Bob Swanson was hoping to take over as producer of his own show after Aces was fired?"

"I cant believe that," Hickman said.

"Why not?"

"Swanson's a lousy producer. I've even hitched about his job as director. This was another example of poor executive power on the part of Max Decker."

"Do you think Swanson could be blackmailing Decker?"

Hickman put away his shotgun. "I doubt it. Max is a powerful man. If he wanted to, he could break Swanson down to a latrine keeper."

"Maybe," I said. "That all depends on whether Swanson saw a certain party dump a quantity of arsenic in a glass two weeks ago. And whether that certain party was Max Decker."

"I—I don't follow you," Hickman stammered.

I smiled. "You should sometime. I'm told it's like watching a cobra about to shed its skin."

Hickman tried to catch my humor but it didn't penetrate. Danny Marble and I climbed down the ladder into the boat.

"Where to?" he asked, "I don't know of any wars that need to be won. How the devil did you manage those three guys anyway?"

"Judo and a little deck wax," I said. "Don't worry. If they'd had an ounce more brains between them we'd have been in trouble, you can bet on that."

The wind was rising cool off the water. "Looks like we might have another storm," Danny said, scanning the sky.

"That's all we need. What time do you go to work on the glass-bottom boat?"

"Soon as the steamer arrives. About twelve-fifteen."

"Could I go down with you?" I asked.

"Sure," Dan said enthusiastically. "So you're a private detective, huh? This ought to be fun."

We landed again at the Pleasure Pier and walked down Crescent Avenue to the Jolly Inn. I wanted to talk to the bartender, Joe King, an old friend of mine from Lake Arrowhead. Joe had been the power behind the bar at The Chalet for many years. He was a dark-complected, nervous type with more ulcers than a sultan has wives.

"What'll you have, Honey gal?" Joe asked.

"A fat man," I said.

"Never heard of one," Joe teased. "What's it made of, vinegar and brandy?"

"Blubber and belly," I corrected. "This one's bald, weighs about three fifty, needs two stools to sit. Seen him around?"

Joe grinned. "Sounds like Max Decker."

I nodded. "When's the last time you saw him?"

"Yesterday afternoon."

"Was he with anyone?"

"Yeah," Joe said. "Cute little doll. He called her Lori, as I remember."

"Smart remembering," I said. "Do you ever watch the Bob Swanson show on TV?"

"Never miss it. Swanson was in here this morning."

"What?"

"About an hour ago. He looked bushed, like he hadn't slept for days."

I practically crawled over the bar. "Did he say anything to you, Joe? About where he's been staying or what he's been doing?"

"He didn't say a word. Just tossed down a double

and walked out. He was pretty dusty. I'd say he'd been on a camping trip or something."

"Thanks, pal. What would private eyes like me do without open-eyed guys like you?"

"Live a little longer," Joe said. "Get out of here! I'd rather associate with alcoholics. At least they're having fun while they're trying to kill themselves."

Outside the Jolly Inn, warm mist dampened the sidewalks as Dan and I headed up the street toward the steamer terminal. The massive white hulk of the channel liner, *Catalina*, was sliding into view around the Casino, its decks jammed with waving, wet tourists.

"Time for us to go to work," Danny said. "What are you going to be looking for?"

"You'll know if I find it" I said. "Come on, let's not miss the boat."

We climbed aboard the glass-bottomed *Phoenix* and Danny took me to a small dressing room. He brought out two sets of long underwear and two orange rubber diving suits.

He smiled embarrassedly. "We usually dive off a tub called *Davey Jones*. She's got separate dressing quarters. Aboard the *Phoenix* this is it, and we don't have time to take turns."

"That's convenient," I said, "for you."

He swallowed a large lump. "I won't look."

"Danny," I said. "I'm a big girl, remember?"

"Yeah," he said uneasily. "That's what I'm trying to forget. I am human, you know!"

"So I noticed back at your cabin."

With his jaw set tight, Danny turned his back and we tugged on our long underwear. After we got into the rubber suits, he looked at me. He, was blushing enough color to paint the Empire State Building.

"The captain wants me to talk to the passengers on the public address system before we go down," Danny said. "I'll introduce you as—Dolores West, a very experienced female skin diver. Do you think you can live up to the fanfare?"

"I'll try."

The *Phoenix*'s paddle wheel was churning us out into the bay by the time Dan and I came up topside in our orange suits. Despite a steady mist, the boat was crammed with eager passengers. We breezed over to a spot near Decker's schooner while Danny did his microphone bit. Then we plunged into the water.

Immediately I became tangled in Iodine Kelp but managed to extract myself with a few healthy kicks of the rubber flippers attached to my feet. Dan pointed out the bright colored fish to a watchful audience while I pretended to search for abalone. But my mind was not on any citizens of the briny deep. I was looking for something man-made; an article a killer might discard as he tossed over Rod's metal case. All that turned up were two soda bottles and a rusted beer can.

It was late afternoon before Dan and I got back to the villa. The sky had opened up into a heavy downpour and we ran all the way from the pier. The poor tourists were in for a foul trip home on the steamer.

I was in for a shock myself. Dan's pals were back

from the mainland, apparently three-sheets-to-the-wind, glassy-eyed and very belligerent. They took one look at me in the tiger-striped swimsuit and growled.

"Danny boy," one bellowed, "you've been holding out on us. Let's spread the wealth."

"This is off-limits," I returned abruptly. "So stop undressing me with your eyes."

"Wow!" howled another. "She's tough. How tough are you, baby?"

Quickly Danny moved in between us. "I'll answer that one," he said. "She's tough enough to send you back to kindergarten, Hank, so take my advice and button your lip."

"Fancy that," Hank retorted. "Even our pal and soul-mate, Danny boy, is getting muscular around the larynx. Perhaps it will be necessary to perform a tonsilectomy, right Arch?"

Arch, a runt with a gutsy-looking face, arched his back. I could see we were going to have trouble. Real trouble. Danny's three friends were feeling no pain, but aching to create a little. It suddenly struck me that there were neither glasses, liquor bottles, nor the smell of alcohol in the small room. These kids were *high*, but from what? They all wore long-sleeve shirts. If there was any possibility they were on heroin, I had to bare their arms to check for needle marks.

"How about a game of strip poker?" I suggested quickly.

Arch unarched and grinned out of the side of his mouth. "Now you're beginning to talk like a lady," he said.

The third member of the clan, a mop-haired brute with buck-teeth, giggled girlishly. "You can say that again. I've got a deck of cards."

Dan flashed me a suspicious look and started to argue with buck-teeth.

"That's fine," I interrupted. "We'll play five-handed, one card apiece. Low man sheds, okay?"

Hank flipped open a card table as the trio grunted favorably. The odds were roughly thirty-to-one against me. One low card and I would lose my tiger stripes. But I wasn't going to leave my fate in the hands of luck.

"I'll deal," Arch said, riffling the deck.

"Wait a minute!" I lifted the cards from his chubby fists. "Low man deals each hand. When I say low, I mean the person with the least amount of clothes. You all have me about seven to one at the moment. It's my deal."

"Okay," buck-teeth agreed. He was shaking so hard he would have agreed to anything. The rest followed suit. Only Danny tried to call off the game, but he was out-voted.

I shuffled, cut and flipped out five cards, face down. "All right," Arch said. "You first Danny boy. Then me, then Hank, then Buck. The lady is last. Go ahead, turn it over."

Dan had a queen. The trio grinned. Arch had a ten. They banged the table happily. Hank had a jack. They clapped each other on the back. Buck had a king. The place nearly flew apart.

"Now it's your turn, blondie," Arch said, licking his chops. "Remember, this was your idea. No sore losers!"

I turned over my card. The trio flattened out.

Ace of spades.

Grumbling bitterly, Arch took off his shoes.

I reshuffled and dealt a new hand. All four had jacks. Arch lined them up in a formidable row.

"Beat that!" he bragged.

I took all four jacks and stacked them one on top of the other. Then I flipped over my card and covered the pile with it. The trio flipped.

Queen of hearts.

All four of them removed a piece of clothing. But no shirts.

I dealt out five more cards. Arch was getting hot around the collar. "This time around," he said, "the lady shows first. We'll reverse the table. I'll show last." I nodded and turned up my card. The trio cackled like a bunch of old hens. Three of diamonds.

Hank had a king. Buck had an eight. Danny had an ace. Arch chuckled and flipped over his card.

Deuce!

Arch was down to his shorts and shirt.

After ten more hands the whole trio was in the same state of undress and I still had my tiger stripes. Danny had lost only his jacket. It was getting so dark, Hank had to turn on the lights.

"Hey, Arch," buck-teeth moaned all of a sudden. "How come we keep losing?"

"I dunno," Arch said. "But I'm beginning to get a pretty good idea. I think the little lady is dealing off the bottom."

Arch demanded the next deal. He shuffled and issued out five cards. I had a bad feeling. Especially since this was the first hand I hadn't dealt—and, as Arch had guessed, off the bottom of the deck.

The trio flipped over their cards. They groaned. Three treys. Dan had a ten of hearts.

My card was a black one. Very black. Deuce! The plan was wrecked. I'd wanted to see a few bare arms. Now they were clamoring to see a few parts of my anatomy.

"Well?" Arch roared, jumping up, "are you going to do it, or should I?"

"I've managed to undress myself since I was five," I said, stalling. "I don't need any lessons now."

"Okay," Hank said impatiently. "Commence!"

The tiger-striped suit was held up by two shoulder straps. I shrugged and unfastened one, edging slowly toward the door. A big storm had turned the early evening pitch black and rain smashed heavily on the roof. The second strap finally gave. Holding up the front of my suit, I eased down the zipper, simultaneously stepping back and grasping the doorknob. Their glazed eyes saw nothing except the fabric easing away from my body as they waited for the unveiling.

As I was about to turn the knob, the lights went out. The cursing and screaming was riotous.

"Who did it?" roared the runt's voice out of pitch blackness. "Who did it? I'll kill 'em! I'll kill 'em!"

"Nobody done it, Arch," boomed back the nasal voice of buck teeth. "It musta been the storm. The electricity is off."

"Well, get it on again!" Arch screamed wildly.

I whirled around, flung open the door and dashed out into the night. Rain drilled in my eyes. I stumbled, snagged my swimsuit on something sharp and tried to break loose. The fabric ripped apart below the zipper as I lunged free. Then a biting chill swept over me. My suit was gone!

I searched frantically for my cabin, but the rain and darkness obliterated everything. A hundred and fifty cabins and they all looked alike. I wound up on a side street, lost, angry and naked. The street was apparently deserted, but I couldn't be sure. Lights were out all over Avalon.

I stopped and listened. Drenching rain pelted against the pavement. There was one other sound, distant and weird. The chimes. They were pealing wildly up on the hillside.

I ran for the police station. It would be embarrassing, but I had no choice.

Chief Clements almost knocked me down in the doorway of the police building. He wore a black slicker and apparently was in a big hurry. He gave me a quick rundown with the flashlight and bellowed, "Miss West, for God's sake, don't you ever wear clothes?"

He swept me into his office and a warm blanket as I explained the circumstances. His face had an expression of exasperation and worry.

"We've been looking for you," Clements said. "Decker's been found."

"Where?" I demanded.

"Up in the chimes tower," the police chief said.

"What was he doing up there?"

Clement wiped a wet hand across his old face. "He was hanging by a thick rope. Decker's dead!"

FOURTEEN

I NEARLY DROPPED MY BLANKET. "HOW'D YOU HAPPEN TO find him up there?"

"The chimes started ringing at five o'clock," Clements said, "and they never stopped. One of the Island Company repair men went to check the trouble. Decker was strung up on a rod that controls the timing device."

"But the electricity," I said. "I thought there was a power failure."

"There is," the police chief explained. "Decker was hung up on a timing rod. His weight created a jam-up in the bell mechanism."

"Where's the body now?"

"In the island morgue. He's had a .38 caliber bullet lodged in his heart. That's what really killed him."

"It must be Swanson," I said, shaking my head. "But it just doesn't add up."

"How big is this TV actor, Swanson?" Clements asked.

"About average. He's in terrific shape, though. Strong as a bull physically."

"That's what I thought."

"I don't get you."

Clements produced a crumpled piece of paper and handed it to me. The typewritten note read, MEET ME IN THE CHIMES TOWER AT FOUR-THIRTY THIS AFTERNOON. VITALLY IMPORTANT. B. S.

I examined the note. "Where'd you get this?"

The old police chief struck the table with a match and applied the flame to his cigarette. "We found it in Decker's coat pocket. Swanson's first name is Bob, isn't it?"

I nodded. This note looked exactly like the one Mark and I had found in Rod Caine's pocket. All capital letters and an unusual typeface. Both messages were probably from the same typewriter. Swanson had a portable in his stateroom aboard *Hell's Light*.

"Any trace of Swanson?" I asked.

"No. The storm's loused us up completely," Clements said. "It's been pretty dusty around the tower. We might have followed his trail if the rain hadn't obliterated everything. I've got men covering the airport and both piers."

Dusty! That coincided with Joe King's description of Swanson. Golden Boy could have investigated the chimes area before sending his message to Decker.

I studied the old police chiefs face, then said, "How would you guess it was done? It's no easy matter to hang a man who weighs three hundred and fifty pounds."

"There's a ledge next to the timing rod," Clements said. "I figure Swanson got Decker up on that ledge at gunpoint, then ordered him to slip on the noose. The bullet did the rest."

Clements loaned me some trousers and a shirt. "I'm going back to *Hell's Light*," I said.

"You want a lift out to the yacht?"

"No thanks, I'll find a way. Do you have a flashlight you can spare?"

The grizzled police officer brought one out of a drawer. "Incidentally," he said, "we still haven't been able to get to the mainland with those thumb impressions from Ann Claypool. All the airstrips are closed over there."

I rolled my eyes dismally. "Listen, Chief, do me a favor. Check Decker's arms for needle marks. He might have been a narcotics addict."

The chimes had stopped and raindrops slackened into a mist by the time I reached the Villa. My footsteps rang loudly on the wooden walkways as I searched for my own cabin. When I found number thirty-six the door was ajar.

Hadn't I locked it? My mind, conflicted with thoughts about Decker's murder, couldn't come up with a positive answer. I stepped inside and closed the door, automatically flicking the wall switch. Nothing happened. The power was still off.

Then a metal instrument flashed in the darkness. I ducked, but not far enough. The weapon caught me on the side of the head just as one of my fingernails tore into something. I crumpled to the floor, rolled over and crawled for the door. A dark figure was stumbling clumsily down the walkway. Struggling to my feet, I started in pursuit, collapsing after a few steps. My head felt like a full-scale assault at Iwo Jima.

When I finally reached the street, it was deserted. My first impulse carried me to the Jolly Inn. Candles flickered on the tables and behind the bar. The place was alive with music, laughter and the jangled chorus of glasses, bottles and people bumping around on the dance floor.

Fighting a blackout, I grabbed the edge of the bar and shot a flare up in the general direction of Joe King. He got my signal and breezed over.

"For God's sake, Honey," Joe said angrily. "You look like Hell-warmed-over for the Fourth-of-July. What's happened?"

"Have you seen Swanson in the last few minutes?" I demanded.

"No. Haven't seen him since this morning."

"You're sure?"

"Of course I'm sure," Joe said. "What are you doing in men's clothes? I hardly recognized you."

"My dressmaker's on vacation!" I said, holding my head. There was a lump on the left side that would have frightened an ostrich. I studied the crowd. The character who leveled me with the blunt instrument had to be around somewhere. And I felt certain that character was Swanson.

I dashed across the street to the Hi-Ho bar. The

same sort of candlelit fandango was going on. One difference. Danny Marble was sitting at a table with a
blonde about my size. One difference here, too. This gal
didn't have a lump on her topside. I joined them.

"Gee, Honey," Danny said warmly, "where you
been? I looked for you." He glanced at his partner. "Oh,
I'd like you to meet Toni."

Toni was about twenty and stacked to the rooftops in
a flashy orange dress.

"I owe you an apology, Danny," I said. "I was sure
your story about another gal was a phony."

The big youth grinned. "Well, I didn't tell you the
absolute truth. I knew you weren't Toni in the first place."

I scanned the surrounding populace. No Swanson.

"Listen, Danny," I said quickly. "Did you go to my
cabin after the card game?"

"Yeah, I was worried. It was raining bad and I knew
you weren't exactly dressed for the weather."

"How'd you know that?"

Danny said, "I found your bathing suit. It was caught
in a fence outside our cabin. So I took it to your place."

"Did you try the door?"

"Sure. But I knocked first."

"Was it unlocked?"

"Yeah, it was," Danny said. "That surprised me, because you weren't there and I saw you lock it when we
left for the *Phoenix*."

"You did see me lock it?"

"Of course. I even tried it after you turned the key.
Don't you remember?"

I nodded dazedly. Blackness was drawing in again and I needed air. Without an explanation, I headed for the street. The night mist felt cool to my face. I walked up one street and down another. More than anything I wanted to come face to face with Robert Swanson, television's gift to humanity. I wanted to take that gift and give it back to the Indians, piece by piece.

I wound up at the police station and quickly phoned the Los Angeles Sheriff's office, homicide.

"We're socked in solid, Honey," Mark explained, after he got on the phone. "I've been trying to charter a plane for the past three hours, but everything's grounded. You might have mist, but we've got the works. Lightning, thunder, hail. It's like pea soup outside."

"You should crawl inside my head," I groaned. "Pea soup doesn't begin to describe the weather conditions. Somebody slugged me."

Mark swore. "I told you to stay out of trouble. What happened?"

I gave him the details and then said, "I suppose you know about Decker?"

"Know about him? Clements had me on the phone for forty-five minutes. Why do you think I've been trying to break every law of aerial navigation to get over there?"

"I thought you wanted to see me," I said miserably, trying to make light of the situation. "Now I know the truth. All you want is to gaze at Decker's body and take notes."

"Whose body do you want me to gaze at? If it's yours, I won't bring a note pad, I'll bring a deck of cards."

"Where'd you hear about that?"

"What difference does it make?" he said. "Next time I find out you've been playing strip poker, I'm going to slap you in the pokey so fast you'll think you came up with seven aces!"

"That does it!" I retaliated. "I'm going out and start the biggest strip-poker game in history. By the time you get here, you'll think Catalina is a nudist camp."

"Is that so?" Mark said, suddenly serious. "You're a sassy blonde with plenty of guts and body, but when it comes to the think department, you've got another think coming."

"What do you mean?"

"You *think* Swanson hit you, right?"

"Right!"

There was a slight crackling pause. "Okay. If your Villa door was open after you locked it earlier, someone must have opened it with a key, right?"

"I—guess so," I stammered. "I never thought about it."

"Of course you never thought about it," Mark said. "Hot heads die young. You've got a brain that's saturated with gasoline."

"Who says so?"

"I do. Someone throws a match and you blow, everytime."

I thought about that with my muddled tank of gasoline. Mark was so right. I had been hurt and gone haywire. Ignited was a better word. I'd blown when the chips were down.

"Okay," I said, "I've just installed some asbestos. Fire away!"

"Check with the manager of the Villa," Mark advised. "If your cabin wasn't broken into, then someone used a key. Maybe Swanson gave a song and dance about being your husband and the manager opened the door."

"Think you're smart, don't you?"

Mark said, "It's easy when you're born that way."

"Very funny," I said. "Well, make a joke out of this. I think I've found a connection between the Nelson case and the four murders over here."

"What's the connection?" the lieutenant barked.

"The metal case containing Rod Caine's lab equipment. I believe it was used to transfer heroin."

"Do you know for sure?"

"No. But I'm going to find out. You'd better break up the atmosphere as soon as you can and get over here before I win that bet of ours by default."

Mark told me to stay out of dark cabins, promised to tear holes in the sky and then hung up. I walked to the manager's office after reaching the Villa and rang the bell. A squat little man clutching a candle came to the door.

"Did you open up cabin thirty-six for someone this afternoon?" I asked.

He stared blankly at the candle, then shook his head. "What about the woman who rented the cabin to me this morning? Maybe she opened it."

"That's my wife," he said. "I'll ask her." He disappeared.

He returned shortly. "Yes, she opened up thirty-six. It was early this evening. About six-thirty or seven. The man said his name was West. Said he was your husband—that you misplaced your key."

"I haven't got a husband. What'd he look like?" The manager's face dropped a foot. "This is terrible. Was something taken? It was raining so hard and my wife probably thought—"

"What'd he look like?" I repeated.

He hurriedly disappeared inside again and returned with his wife, a dumpy blonde in a faded negligee.

"What are you trying to start anyway?" she bellowed. "You were with the man when I gave him the key."

I tried to unscramble that one.

She continued, "I don't give out no keys unless the renter is there, and you were there. Now what do you say to that?"

"What was I wearing?"

The dumpy one chewed for an instant on a fingernail. "A raincoat and hat, and—and an orange dress. I seen it under the coat."

"What'd the man look like?"

"Hard to say. He was wearing a trench coat and hat. I never got a good look at his face. He had a lot of pimples, that's all I saw."

"That's enough," I said. "Thanks."

I bent into the wind as I walked down the main street again. Rain drove in under my jacket, drenching my skin.

They were still sitting at the table in the Hi-Ho bar.

I crossed over and plumped down beside blonde, busty Toni. She did resemble me in many respects. I studied Danny's pockmarked cheeks.

"Did you open my cabin door tonight?" I asked him carefully.

"Yeah, I told you," Danny said. "The door was already unlocked."

"Who unlocked it?"

"I dunno."

"The manager's wife down at the Villa says you unlocked it, Danny."

"She's crazy!"

"She says I was with you at the time."

"Well, now you know she's crazy for sure," Danny said.

I glanced at the other blonde. "Except it wasn't me she saw, was it, Danny? It was Toni."

"Does that make sense?"

"No, it doesn't," I said. "That's why I want to know why you did it."

Danny looked at Toni and swallowed hard. "The manager's wife is wrong." He got to his feet. "We better go, Toni."

I shoved the kid into his chair. "Now, listen, mister," I said, "someone was waiting for me inside my cabin tonight when I got back. He didn't care about playing strip poker or diving for abalone, he just wanted to split my skull in half. And he would have done it if I hadn't dodged. Now, why'd you open that door, Danny?"

"I didn't!"

"You wanted that metal case back. You wanted to be absolutely certain you hadn't left any heroin caps inside, didn't you?"

Danny got to his feet. "You're crazy!"

I pushed him down again and reached for his right shirt sleeve. "Show me your arms. Danny!"

"No!" He pulled away.

I grasped Toni's left arm and straightened it out. In the slender white hollow was a blue vein, punctured with tiny, dark needle marks.

"Now what do you say, Danny?"

"That doesn't prove anything. Now leave us alone!"

"You were in my cabin, weren't you?"

"No!"

"You're a liar. Who's supplying you with junk? Swanson?"

"Na!"

"Who?"

"Nobody! I didn't open your door. I wasn't in your cabin."

I kicked his chair and Danny went head-over-heels into another table. Chairs, people, food, glasses and candles went hurtling every which way. The Hi-Ho bar seemed to rise up in one stupendous wave and break for the front door. In the wild excitement two people vanished into the night rain—Danny Marble and blonde Toni.

I could have kicked myself I was so mad. Nothing was damaged in the Hi-Ho except my hopes for a quick solution to the cabin attack. Mark was absolutely right.

My temper always got the better of me at the wrong time.

Outside, the street lights went on and the rain stopped. I returned to my cabin, made certain the metal case was gone, then climbed the long flight of steps to the chimes tower.

The hillside area, above the dark, dimly lit city, seemed deserted until the crunch of footsteps rose behind me. I whirled. A big shape loomed up in the darkness. I caught the man in the glare of my flashlight. It was Rod Caine.

He wore a sleeveless shirt and on the lower part of his right arm was a long, deep scratch.

FIFTEEN

"**R**OD! WHAT ARE YOU DOING ON THIS ISLAND?"

"Honey, am I glad to see you alive," he said, trying to put his arms around me.

I stepped back. "I told you to stay aboard *Hell's Light*. Why didn't you?"

He frowned at my cool reception. "I got a message."

"You were supposed to ignore any messages." I stared at the slash on his forearm.

Rod shook his head. "This one I couldn't ignore. It was from Bob Swanson, a note saying he was going to kill you."

"Where is it?"

He shrugged his big shoulders. "I don't know. I guess I lost it. It shook me up so much I just hopped a water taxi and came on into Avalon. Thank God you're all right."

"Who delivered the message?"

"It came by the same water taxi," he said, irritated by my questions. "What's the matter?"

"What time'd you arrive in Avalon?"

"I don't know. Four-thirty. Five. What difference does it make?"

"It makes a big difference," I said. "Max Decker was murdered around that time."

"Yeah," Rod winced. "I heard about Max. Too bad."

"Who'd you hear it from?"

"Chief Clements. He told me you were staying in number thirty-six at the Villa. I went there. The door was open, but nobody was around, so I finally came up here."

"What time did you see Chief Clements?"

"About two hours ago," Rod said. "What is this, anyway? Am I a suspect again?"

"Where'd you get that scratch on your arm?" Rod looked at the long deep wound. "I got mixed up with a woman. Does that answer your question, Miss District Attorney?"

I took a firm hold on the butt of the flashlight. "I never thought you'd do anything like this."

"Like what?" Rod's nostrils flared angrily. "If you must know the truth, Lori scratched me with her fingernails. We got into an argument about you. She got mad and drew blood. Is that what you're talking about?"

"When did this happen?"

"About an hour before I received the message from Swanson. Lori wound up with a black eye, but I had to do it. She would have cut me to ribbons. What's this all about?"

"Is Lori still aboard *Hells Light*?"

"As far as I know she is," Rod said. "I don't think she'd travel far with an eye like that."

"All right," I said, "let's go see her."

I started down the path toward town. Rod stopped me abruptly. "What difference does it make if Lori has a shiner? I didn't mean to hurt her. What's the matter with you?"

I studied him in the glare of the flashlight. "If Lori Aces doesn't have a black eye, or if she's gone, Rod, you're in trouble. Big trouble. Understand?"

"No, I don't. What the hell is this? I came into Avalon to help you; is this the thanks I get?"

"I don't know what kind of thanks you're looking for," I said, "but whatever it is, you'll get it. I'll see to that personally."

We walked down the long flight of steps. I checked with the water-taxi service. There was no record of a message being delivered to *Hell's Light*, but the log did show a boat had gone out to Aces' yacht around four o'clock. Chief Clements, several policemen and a half-dozen Coast Guardsmen were on the pier. I asked the police officer whether Rod Caine had reported to the police station and the chief confirmed the incident.

"It was about an hour before you came back and phoned Lieutenant Storm in Los Angeles," Clements said.

I gave the police chief a description of Danny Marble, his girl friend, Toni, and the three strip-poker players.

"If you find them, hold all five on suspicion of narcotics possession." I glanced at Rod and added, "They might lead us to the murderer."

On the water taxi out to *Hell's Light*, Rod was ominously quiet. I wanted to check one phase of his story—Lori Aces' black eye.

My mind kept searching for a connection between the murderer and Danny Marble. Had the metal case actually been found in the bay by the kid? This was a vital question. So was the whereabouts of the boys from the strip-poker game. The manager had said they'd checked out "in a hurry" around the time I'd left the card game. Their cabin, stripped to the pare furniture, revealed no evidence of narcotics.

Rod interrupted my thoughts. "I overheard your conversation with Chief Clements. What's Danny Marble got to do with all this?"

"You know him?" I asked.

"Sure. He's played a lot of tough-kid parts in TV films. I've seen him around Television Riviera. He pals around with a hype named Toni Scortt."

"A voluptuous blonde with blue eyes?"

"Yeah, that's the one," Rod said. "They were great pals with Sam Aces. Sam gave Marble a couple of bits in the Swanson series. Toni likes to act, too, when she isn't on the needle."

"How friendly are they with you?" I asked.

"We say 'hello,' that's all. I dated Toni once, about a year ago. I headed for the nearest exit when she brought out her little kit and a handful of caps."

"Is Marble a user?" I demanded.

"I don't know. I don't think so. He's always been a heavy drinker. The two don't usually go together."

"Rod, did you have any hypodermic needles in your lab case?"

"Sure. Why? You don't think I take junk, do you? Here, look." He held out his arms. They were unmarked except for the scratch on his right forearm.

The gleaming white hull of *Hell's Light* became visible through the mist and spray. Carruthers was on the float to help steady the taxi as Rod and I climbed out. We thanked the old man and proceeded to the main deck.

Lori Aces was not in the swimming pool. We checked her cabin. We searched up forward, the stern, the lower deck, the engine room.

"She's somewhere," Rod said. "She's got to be, unless she left the ship."

"That's possible." I glanced over the railing. "How many feet to the bottom?"

He caught my arm. "Don't be funny. I don't like that kind of joke."

"I don't like the kind of joke someone played on me back at Avalon. It was a lead-pipe cinch to fold me into all kinds of laughter, but I dodged the punch line."

Rod gritted his teeth. "Honey, you burn me right to the ground. Make sense or quit beating your gums."

I twisted his forearm to reveal the long scratch. "Who gave you that?"

"Lori! How many times do I have to tell you?"

"You're lying!"

"I'm not lying!"

I held up my left hand and pointed to the index finger. The nail was torn off to the quick. "It's my hunch," I said, "this nail did the trick."

"You're crazy!"

"You were in cabin thirty-six in the Villa, weren't you?"

Rod swallowed. "Yes, but—"

"Somebody swung at me in the dark and I clawed him with my fingernail. How do you explain the coincidence?"

"I—I don't know. But Lori can explain—"

"Did anyone see you and Lori tangle?" I demanded.

"No. We were in her cabin."

"Did you make any noise?"

"She screamed when I hit her." He opened the front of his shirt revealing deep scratches across his chest. "Do you want to credit yourself with these, too?"

I winced. It looked like the work of a wildcat. "I'm sorry, Rod. I wanted to believe you, but the coincidence was just too much for me."

He said, "Would you call this the luck of Swanson? Even when he doesn't try, the evidence still comes up with my name on it."

"What do you think's happened to Lori Aces," I asked. He started aft. "That's what I'd like to know. Maybe she went to my place. I'm sure she didn't see me leave on the water taxi."

We checked with the people in the bar. Nobody remembered seeing Lori since lunch. Rod got a pair of binoculars and peered through the mist at the shore.

"I think there's a light," he said, lowering the glasses.

"But I can't be sure. It's pretty hazy out there."

"Let's go look," I said. "I'd still like to hear Lori's side of the story."

Rod shook his head. "I think you were born skeptical. Come on!"

We started for the float, then he stopped abruptly. "Have you got your .32 along for protection," he asked.

"Naturally," I said. "You don't think I'd trust you entirely, do you?"

"Of course not," Rod grumbled. "I just wanted to make sure."

Rod's cabin cruiser wasn't tied up at the float. I asked him if Lori might have taken it.

"Nope. I ran the cruiser over to the cave when the blow started up this afternoon. I was afraid if the storm got as bad as it did a couple of days ago, she'd be knocked galley west."

"How'd you get back?"

"Carruthers followed me over in one of the putters."

We climbed into a small boat and started toward shore.

I tried to unlock this case as we cut through the dark waters. Lori Aces had one of several keys. She could definitely eliminate Rod Caine from the cabin attack. But, more than that, she could explain the significance of her meeting with Max Decker in the Jolly Inn bar the same day Aces' blood-stained jacket was found at Little Harbor. I had a hunch Lori held the major key to the whole case. But whether she'd turn it for me was another matter.

Then there was Danny Marble. A clever kid. A very

clever kid. He'd probably known all along who I was. He held a big key. Maybe the most important one. He was getting paid off to pull a few stunts and, obviously, the payoff man was the killer. Was it Swanson? There were only three logical suspects left. Golden Boy, Rod Caine and Lori Aces.

I glanced at Rod out of the corner of my eye. I knew this was the work of a very clever dangerous maniac. This fact bothered me plenty. The finger of suspicion pointed all too clearly at Bob Swanson.

Rod veered the boat into the cave and we stepped out. His own cruiser was raised out of the water on its pulleys. As we walked up the path to the cabin, I had a raw feeling in the pit of my stomach. A kerosene lamp burned in the living room.

Rod opened the front door. "Lori? Lori, where are you?"

No answer. We looked through the house. In the bedroom we found a pile of feminine garments. A sweater. dark slacks, a small bra, panties and high heels. They belonged to Lori Aces.

Rod picked up the shoes. "I don't get it," he said, shaking his head. "She was wearing this stuff the last time I saw her."

I walked outside and checked the grounds. When I returned Rod was still studying the shoes. I lighted a cigarette and sat down.

"Let's conjure up a vision, pal," I said. "Where is she, taking a midnight swim in the nude?"

"I—I don't know," Rod stammered.

"I suppose you noticed there weren't any other boats down below. What do you make of that?"

Rod tossed the shoes on the bed and threw up his hands. "I tell you I don't know. Honey, believe me, I'm as much in the dark about this thing as you are."

"If you saw there were no other boats, why'd you call her name when you walked in?"

"There was a light," Rod said. "I did it instinctively."

"You do a lot of things instinctively, don't you?"

"No," he said angrily. "I don't kill instinctively, if that's what you mean!"

"How do you kill, Rod?"

"I don't!"

He stormed into the living room, poured a shot of whiskey and slugged it down non-stop.

"You want one?" he asked, holding up the bottle.

I shook my head.

Nervously, he poured again, spilling some on the floor. "What gives you the idea Lori's dead?" he asked.

"I didn't say I thought she was."

Rod gulped down another shot and wiped off his mouth with the back of his hand. "Cut the doubletalk," he said. "Maybe she is out for a swim. Lori's always been cracked on swimming in the raw."

"So I understand. But where's the boat that brought her here?"

"Maybe she swam from *Hell's Light*."

"She swam nearly a mile in high heels?"

Rod set the bottle down hard. "I told you, I don't know!"

"Well, I do. She couldn't have done it unless she carried the shoes in her teeth."

He threw himself in a chair and groaned. "All right. If the merry-go-round ring fits, I'll wear it. I guess we've been working up to this, haven't we?"

"I don't know," I said. 'That's a question you'll have to answer.

"Okay," Rod said, "I'll answer it. Maybe I am a pigeon for Aces and Meeler and Decker. But what about Ann Claypool? I couldn't have done that one. We were together the whole time."

I pulled out the .32 and leveled it at him. "Were we, Rod? I thought about that while I was in Avalon. Remember, you heard someone running outside my cabin. You disappeared for a few minutes. Long enough to stop off for a short visit with little Ann. Long enough to—"

"No!" Rod got to his feet. "For God's sake, Honey, what would I want to kill Ann Claypool for? Or Aces or Meeler or Decker? I didn't like Sam, true, but Meeler was my friend. And as for Max Decker or Ann Claypool, I had nothing against either of them. Maybe I disliked Sam Aces enough to want to kill him, but I didn't kill him! And the other three—sure, they had their bad points—but so do I."

"I'd like to believe you, Rod," I said softly. "But there are only two people now who can possibly clear you in this mess—Lori Aces and Bob Swanson."

Rod paced around the room nervously. Finally, he stopped and stared at me. "Look, Honey! Lori Aces may be mired up with Swanson in this business. If she is, I'm in trouble! Don't you understand? They could vanish. Head for South America and hole up for ten years if they wanted to. And where would that leave me?"

"In a gas chamber," I said.

"Yeah, that's right!" Rod retorted. "And don't think these clothes of Lori's and anything else Swanson wants to plant around the island, won't contribute to sending me there."

He picked up the whiskey bottle, juggled it an instant and then swung it hard in my direction. Glass and whiskey sprayed in all directions. So did the gun. Before I had a chance to pick up the right piece of merchandise, Rod had the revolver in his hand and was pointing it straight at my middle.

"I'm sorry to have to do this, Honey," he said, "but you leave me no choice."

I stood my ground, tight as a drum. "If you didn't kill anyone, you have nothing to worry about. Give me the gun."

"Not this trip, baby," Rod said. "I'm the guy with the merry-go-round ring, remember? That entitles me to a free ride to the gas chamber. Only I'm not accepting the prize."

"You'd never die for something you didn't do!"

Rod smiled unhappily. "Sing that lullaby in church, Honey. You'll get a better collection."

"What do you plan to do?"

"Get out of here," Rod answered. "I can take a piece of that South America bit myself. I'm not proud. Maybe I'll run across two old friends of mine. If I do, I'll send

you back their skulls—after I shrink them down to size."
He started for the door.

"Running away won't help, Rod. That's what
Swanson wants, don't you see? You'll never clear yourself this way. He could turn up in a week with lily white
hands and an iron-clad alibi. And when the police caught
you, you'd hang for sure. You can bet on that."

Rod said grimly, "Either way, I've had it." He
reached the doorway. "Now take my advice. Don't come
down that path for at least fifteen minutes. I like life and
I don't plan to give it up for anyone, understand?"

I nodded half-heartedly, and he was gone. I considered several plans to stop him, but discarded them all. If
Rod Caine were the murderer, he wouldn't hesitate to
add me to the score.

If he weren't, it didn't really matter if he escaped. I
was certain he'd turn up sooner or later.

I examined Rod's portable typewriter, a brand new
Royal with a blue chassis. I fed a piece of paper into
it. The type was distinctive. I recognized it immediately.
It had exactly the same characteristics as the type on the
notes found in Rod Caine's and Max Decker's coat
pockets.

I entered his bedroom again and checked the closets
and bureau drawers. Then I looked under the bed.

A battered nude body stared sightlessly at me.

SIXTEEN

SWEET CHILDLIKE LORI WAS A NIGHTMARE. SHE'D BEEN viciously beaten to death and there were bruises all over her body.

I pulled her out from under the bed. There were several needle marks in the crook of her arm. I shook my head dismally. Apparently she had been a narcotic addict. Now there'd be no more fixes. No more caps or spoons or needles. Lori Aces had met with the same violent end that had taken five others, including Herb Nelson.

It made me sick inside just to look at her.

I walked down the hill to the cave. Rod had taken the small boat. I lowered his cabin cruiser into the swell, climbed into the pilot's seat, fired up the engines and steered her into the open sea.

After tying up the cruiser at the yacht's float, I went aboard *Hells Light* and down to B Deck. The watertight door leading into the liquor-supply room was open. I walked inside and turned on the light. Above, in the swimming-pool bar, noise, clinking glasses and confusion reigned as usual.

Several cases of liquor were dumped on their sides and heelmarks indicated that they had been split open from repeated blows of a heavy shoe or boot. Bottles of scotch rolled loosely on the floor of the storeroom.

I searched through the cardboard debris. Then I found what I was looking for. A small heroin cap. In a still unopened case there were a dozen more caps and two hypodermic kits. Nearby, a handkerchief was caught under one of the broken cases. The piece of silk bore the initials L.A.

Mark Storm arrived aboard *Hell's Light* about an hour after I discovered the heroin cache. He was accompanied by Chief Clements, two Avalon policemen, a Coast Guard commander and three other officers. They escorted a very tired, dusty, ominously silent prisoner in handcuffs. Rod Caine.

I took Mark aside, showed him the heroin caps and told him about Lori Aces. The big lieutenant rolled with the punch, grimly wiped a hand across his eyes and swore.

"Honey," Mark said, "this guy's a maniac. It's a wonder he didn't get you in the bargain."

"Where'd you find him?" I asked.

"A couple of Clements' men caught him on the hillside near the old Wrigley home."

"What was he doing there, Mark?"

"Burying a metal case full of lab equipment."

They took Rod into the yacht's dining room for questioning. Two other men from the L. A. Sheriff's office joined the group as Mark began the interrogation. Rod said he had gone into Avalon to search for Swanson.

"Why?" Mark asked.

"Swanson's been trying to swing me for these murders. I had to find him to clear myself."

"Did you find him?" Clements demanded.

"No."

"What were you doing up near the Wrigley home?" Rod glowered angrily. "Looking for my stolen gear." Clements said, "When you were apprehended by two of my officers, they claim you were trying to bury a metal case containing some instruments."

"That's crazy!" Rod said. "I got a tip from one of Danny Marble's pals that a case with my initials was buried up on the hillside. He drew a map for me and I went to get it."

"Where's the map?" Mark demanded.

Rod shook his head. "I don't know. I guess in the excitement of the arrest, I lost it."

Mark bent toward the handcuffed man. "You have a great faculty for losing important evidence, haven't you, Mr. Caine?"

"No! Anyway, what's so important about a map? I told you the truth. I was digging up the case, not burying it."

"Why?"

"It substantiated part of my original story," Rod said. "I used the equipment to analyze the liquid in Sam Aces' glass. The case and contents were stolen. I wanted to get them back to prove I wasn't lying."

"How did you get to Avalon?" Clements asked. "In a putter. I went as far as the old seaplane airport and then swam ashore. I suppose you found the boat?"

"Yeah, we did," Mark said carefully. "When's the last time you saw Bob Swanson?"

Rod wiped a nervous hand across his face. "Let's see. Thursday morning. The day he disappeared. Two days ago."

"You're sure of this?"

"Absolutely. I wouldn't have been looking for him last night if I'd seen him since then."

Mark lit a cigarette and regarded Rod carefully. "When's the last time you saw Lori Aces?"

Rod pursed his lips. "Yesterday afternoon. We had a fight. I walked out and haven't seen her since."

"You're certain?"

"Of course I am. Did you ever find her?"

"Yes, we did," Mark said quietly. "Or rather Miss West found her."

"Where?"

"Where you left her," Mark continued casually.

"You mean in her stateroom," Rod said.

"No. Under the bed in your island cabin."

Rod shot to his feet "Are you crazy? She's not—dead?"

"I think you can answer that one."

"No!" Rod exclaimed, shaking his head. "No, no, no! Lori can't be dead! She shouldn't be dead."

Mark said, "You're right this time. You just kicked a little too hard."

Rod slumped back in his chair. "You—you got this all wrong. I hit her, yes, but I never kicked her. I never struck her more than once, believe me.

"Where was the argument?"

"Lori's stateroom."

"What time?"

"Around two o'clock."

"Want me to tell you exactly how it happened?" Mark said quickly. "You and she were in this together. You were afraid Lori would crack pretty soon, weren't you, Caine? You knew she had a monkey on her back and couldn't be trusted, so you took her to your cabin on the island and beat her up."

"No!"

"You knocked her down and kicked her to death."

Rod lashed, "You're crazy!"

"Then you stuffed her under your bed until you decided how to dispose of the body."

"No! For God's sake!"

"We found blood stains on a shirt and a pair of pants that belong to you.

"That was from me," Rod said. "She ripped me to pieces. But Lori didn't bleed. Don't you understand? Swanson did this. He's trying to frame me.

"That alibi won't work any more," Mark said tightly.

"What do you mean?"

"We've found him."

Rod's eyes blazed. "Where is he? That dirty, rotten bastard. I'll kill him!"

Mark looked at Chief Clements and shook his head unhappily. Then he grabbed Caine angrily by the shoulders, lifting him out of his chair. "You're a card, aren't you, Caine? Why don't you spit it out? We found Bob Swanson about a half-hour before you were apprehended. He was lying on the rocks below the chimes tower. He has a bullet smack between his eyes and he's dead! He's about as dead as you are, brother, believe me!"

Rod Caine folded up like a collapsible toy.

I nearly fainted. Mark hadn't said one word to me about finding Swanson's body.

"I've had it," Rod groaned miserably. "Really had it!"

"You should have pushed harder," Mark said. "If he'd hit the water, it's possible he'd never been found. Your story always was pretty thin, but with Swanson missing indefinitely it might have held up."

Rod glanced at me, his mouth twisted horribly. "Why'd you do it, Caine?" Mark asked. "Mass murder is serious business."

The handcuffed writer was silent for a long moment, his breathing punctuating the air like a rapid-fire shotgun. Then he broke, "I didn't do it!"

Mark cocked his hat back on his head. "You said you were being framed. That Swanson was framing you. Swanson was shot hours before Lori Aces was murdered. Now, how did he frame that one?"

"I don't know! I don't know how anything could have happened!"

"You don't expect us to believe that!"

"I don't know what I expect you to believe, but I didn't do it!"

Mark demanded, "You did have reason to kill Sam Aces, didn't you?"

"Not exactly, no!"

"He disfigured your face, didn't he?"

Rod leaned forward in his chair, cupping his face in his hands. "A little," he whispered. "But I didn't want to kill him for it."

"Joe Meeler took your job on the Swanson show," Mark continued to hammer, "isn't that right?"

"Yes, but I was glad Joe got the job," Rod said. "He was my friend."

Mark paced around the room for a moment, then he said, "You hated Ann Claypool, didn't you?"

"No!"

Wince Claypool was your friend in college, wasn't he? You told him to stay away from Ann, but he refused. He married her while you two were in business together. She destroyed that business, didn't she?"

Rod was on the ropes and reeling. He swayed back in his chair. "Yes—yes, in a way she did, but she wasn't the only reason we folded. Vince drank a lot. He kept digging into the till—"

"He drank because of Ann, didn't he?" Mark argued hotly.

"I guess so.—"

"You hated her for that!"

"Yes— No! I didn't really hate her—I—"

Mark continued, "You knew what kind of man Max Decker was, didn't you?"

"What do you mean?"

"Ruthless, hard, scheming," Mark drilled. "You said right here, aboard this ship, that Decker would go to almost any lengths to crush someone, didn't you?"

"I've said that a lot of times."

"Did he ever try to crush you?"

Rod twisted miserably in his chair. "He's tried to ruin a dozen people."

"Did he ever try to ruin you?"

"Yes!" Rod exclaimed. "But that's all part of this rotten game. That's why I got out of it. It's cut-throat! They'll shrink your head down to a walnut and crack it if they get half the chance!"

Mark surveyed the group. Clements shook his head as if to say, This guy's as loco as they come! The chief asked Rod, "Where's the .38 you used on Decker and Swanson?"

"I haven't got a .38," Rod said.

"Did you throw that in the ocean along with Swanson's body?"

"No!"

Clements produced a .32 and handed it to me. "This is your revolver, isn't it, Miss West?"

I nodded.

"Caine was carrying it when my men tagged him on the hillside," Clements continued. He studied

Rod's haggard face. "Did you use this weapon on Sam Aces?"

Rod tried to rise out of his chair. "I never fired that weapon in my life!" He slumped back and looked at me. "Believe me, Honey, I only took the gun because I knew you'd use it to bring me in."

Mark got to his feet again. "You faked that message to Decker from Swanson, didn't you?"

"I don't know what message you're talking about," Rod said.

'The one where Swanson said he'd meet Decker in the chimes tower yesterday at four-thirty."

"I didn't send any such message," Rod argued. "I got one myself signed by Swanson. That's why I went into Avalon. Swanson said he was going to kill Honey."

Mark leaned over Rod. "Where is this message?"

"I—I don't know."

Mark studied the group for an instant, then turned his eyes on Rod again. "Miss West says you met her up at the chimes tower last night, is that correct?"

"Yes," Rod said. "I was worried about her. I heard about Decker, went to her cabin and when I found she was gone I went up to the tower."

"Or was it this way?" Mark hurled. "After murdering Decker and Swanson, you went to Honey's cabin to look for your case which, before it was stolen, had contained heroin caps for your confederate, Lori Aces. Honey walked in. You hit her with the butt of your gun and ran. But she managed to scrape your arm with her fingernail; isn't that nearer to the truth?"

"No! I told you Lori did this to my arm. If you want further proof, look at this!"

Rod opened his shirt to reveal the long, hideous marks on his chest.

"You know what I think?" Mark said. "I think you did that yourself."

"Are you crazy? Why would I?"

"Because you knew Honey would remember inflicting the wound on your arm. You remembered your argument with Lori, so you hauled off with your own fingernails and raked yourself."

"Run a test on Lori's fingernails then!" Rod said hotly. "You'll find bits of me under every one of them."

Mark grinned. "Maybe we will, Caine, but that won't prove a thing. Naturally, if you beat the hell out of her she was bound to get you a couple of times.

Rod slumped over in his seat and ran the cool hardness of the handcuffs over his forehead. "Like I said," he moaned dismally, "I've had it! You've really got me."

"You can say that again!" Mark taunted. "You shot and killed Swanson because you hated his guts for not reinstating you with the show."

"He signed me to a contract," Rod argued. "He wanted me back on the show. The contract must be filed somewhere in his office at Television Riviera."

Mark shook his head. "No such luck, boy. We went over his office with a fine-tooth comb. There's no contract with your signature on it anywhere."

"I—I don't get this," Rod stammered. "It all falls into place, I know, but I didn't do it. Someone's clever—"

"You, Caine," Mark interrupted. "You were the clever one. Up to a point. You made it look like Swanson. You were framing him and saying all along that he was framing you. But you made two major mistakes. Pushing Swanson's dead body off the cliff at low tide was one of them. And the other—you fought too hard with Ann Claypool when you drowned her in the bathtub."

"I didn't drown her!"

Mark glanced at me. "The coroner's official verdict was death by drowning, not strangulation." Then he crossed to Clements. "Chief, could I have those blowups now, please."

Clements removed two photographs from a brief-case and handed them to Mark. The lieutenant showed them around the room, finally ending with Rod Caine.

"These are enlargements of the thumbprints taken from the neck of Ann Claypool," Mark said. "They match the prints we took from you exactly. Now what do you say, Mr. Caine?"

"Okay," Rod murmured, head hung low, unable to look up at the undeniable evidence of the enlarged thumbprints. "I'll tell you the truth."

"It's about time," Mark said, surveying the group. He smiled triumphantly at my stunned expression.

"You're right," Rod continued. "Those are my prints, but I didn't murder Ann Claypool. I—I was in Honey's cabin. We were talking about Joe Meeler when we heard a sound outside."

"What kind of sound?" Mark growled.

"Somebody running on deck," Rod explained. "It

came like a volley of shots. Honey'll back me up on this. I went out to see who it was. The sound lead me to Ann's cabin. The door was open a little, so I went in. It had been Ann all right. She was wet and out of breath. I asked her what was going on. She was drunk. She shouted at me to mind my own business. I told her it was my business. She'd tricked me earlier into going to my island cabin on the ruse that Bob Swanson was there waiting to talk to me. I demanded the truth, but she ordered me out. I guess I got excited. She tried to push me out the door and I grabbed her by the throat. Believe me, I didn't strangle her. She tried to scream and I threw her over the bed and walked out. The next time I saw her she was in the bathtub—dead."

Mark said, "I'm surprised, Caine. Being a writer I thought you'd come up with a better story than that."

"It's the truth, believe me," Rod pleaded.

"I don't buy it," Mark said. "And I don't think anyone else here does either." He stared into Rod's sullen eyes. "You're the last man standing, Caine. You eliminated every possible suspect except yourself. Maybe you even got Herb Nelson. If you did, that makes seven. And if you could have nailed Honey it would have been eight. A nice round number in any man's language. Especially in the tongue of a psychopathic killer."

The lieutenant gestured at one of the men from the sheriff's office. Together they lifted Rod Caine out of his chair and started him toward the door.

I went after them, whispering, "Mark, you got the wrong man. I'm sure you have."

"Are you kidding?" he said. "Don't you believe in evidence?"

"Sure, but—"

"You're just sore because you lost your bet."

We reached the end of the dining room. Mark opened the door.

Outside on deck, his face illuminated by starboard rail lights, stood Sam Aces.

SEVENTEEN

SAM HELD HIS LEFT HAND BEHIND HIS BACK. THERE was blood on his white shirt and he weaved as he stumbled toward the door, a pained expression around his mouth.

I rushed to him, slipping his arm around my shoulders.

"I'm hurt, Honey," he whispered. "I didn't think I'd make it."

While I helped Sam into the dining roam, Mark had one of the deputies remove Rod Caine to another part of the ship.

For an instant, Rod and Sam surveyed each other in the doorway, then Chief Clements helped me ease Sam Aces into a chair. He cried out from the pain, staggered to his feet, pushed several helping hands away and crumpled to the floor. In the middle of his back was a bullet hole.

"Get a doctor, quick!" I yelled at Chief Clements.

Mark rolled Sam over and said, "Who did it, Aces?"

"I—it must have been Caine," the lanky producer whispered. "I didn't see him. He got me through the window from behind. I fell and didn't move for a long time. I guess he thought I was dead."

I wiped a trickle of blood out of the corner of his mouth with my handkerchief. "Where did it happen, Sam?"

"In a little house we rented near the chimes tower."

"What do you mean we, Sam?"

"Swanson and I. We—we were trying to outsmart Caine. But I guess he was much smarter than we figured." Aces choked, gasped desperately for breath.

Mark leaned over the wounded man. "Aces, we've sent for a doctor—"

"It—it's too late for that," Sam whispered. "I got to tell you something. I—I came all this way because—because you got to know the—truth."

"All right, Aces, tell us as much as you can." Sam closed his eyes for an instant and said, "I—I've been handling narcotics. The yacht's loaded with heroin. Caps are packed in liquor cases down in the storeroom."

"Why, Sam?" I asked. "You didn't need the money. You don't take the stuff. Why'd you fool with it?"

The producer shook his head and groaned. "It was Lori. She was an addict when I married her. I didn't know. When I caught her taking junk she threatened to leave me if I didn't help her get the stuff. I—I couldn't let her go. I love Lori. I love her more than anything else in the world."

I glanced at Mark. It was obvious Sam Aces didn't know his wife was dead.

"To save my marriage," he continued, "I got involved. It wasn't much at first. Then the big operators backed me against the wall. They—they threatened to ruin me if I didn't cooperate. They turned *Hell's Light* into a floating warehouse and forced me to supply the pushers."

"Herb Nelson was one of your clients, wasn't he?" Mark said.

"Yes."

"Do you know who murdered him?"

"No."

"Why did you hire me, Sam?" I asked.

Aces peered up at me, his eyes glazed with pain. "Because—because I couldn't go to the police. They might have traced down my narcotics connections. But I had to know who was trying to poison me."

"You were searching for something that day in my office, weren't you, Sam?"

"Yes."

"Was it Herb Nelson's file?"

"Yes. I was afraid you had some information about his being a pusher that might lead to me."

"Do you know who stole my gun?" I asked.

Aces tried to smile. "I took it, Honey."

"Why?"

"I—I got scared. I wanted you to quit the case. You were much too smart. But—I knew you'd only be more suspicious if I fired you. So, I took your gun out of your bag."

"And took two shots at me."

Aces winced. "Yes. I only meant to frighten you, but you moved at the wrong moment. I—I was very sorry about that."

Mark said, "Did you really believe Swanson was trying to poison you?"

"Yes."

"You said you and Swanson rented a cabin together in Avalon. When did you change your mind about him?"

"The night I disappeared."

"What happened that night?"

"I—I faked the poisoning," Aces said, struggling for his words. "I wanted to confuse Swanson, bring him into the open. Let him trap himself. But, I was wrong. B.S. wasn't the guy who was after me. I realized that after somebody cracked him on the skull and hung him from the ceiling in Honey's cabin."

I wiped another trickle of blood from Aces' mouth. "You hid in that trunk up on the bow, didn't you, Sam?"

"Yes," Aces whispered. "Then later I moved down below to a place you never would have found. There's a false bulkhead on the stern end of the engine room."

"You were bleeding," Mark said. "We found blood stains in the bow trunk. What happened?"

Aces tried to smile again. "I saw red when B.S. came into the bar and started swinging at Rod Caine. You remember, Honey. I hit him pretty hard with my fist." He held up his right hand. His knuckles were lacerated. "Lucky it was raining," he added, staring at me, "or you could have followed my trail straight to that trunk."

"Then what?"

The wounded producer lifted up slightly, groaning from new pain. Finally, he said, "We—decided Rod Caine was our man."

"Who's we? You and Swanson?"

"No."

"Who?"

"I—I can't tell you," Aces said lowly. "I met with B.S. during the night—down in the secret room. I told him Caine was out to get us both. He was skeptical, but agreed to help me find out. The next morning we went to Caine's island cabin. We planted a note in his coat pocket and then took my jacket to Little Harbor."

"You smeared it with blood, put a bullet hole through the front and dumped the jacket on the beach," I said.

"Yes. We wanted to cast suspicion on Caine so the police would take him into custody after finding the note and the jacket."

I added, "Then Bob Swanson actually did order Ann Claypool to send Caine to his island cabin for a meeting."

Aces nodded.

"This was supposed to attract us into following Caine and searching for his cabin."

"Yes."

"And Swanson's disappearance on the beach at White's Landing was another ruse.

"Yes. He met me at a secret cove and we went into Avalon to the house near the chimes tower."

"Who made the arrangements for the rental?" Mark asked.

"Danny Marble."

"Does he work for you?"

Aces said, "He's a pusher. He handles the young island crowd during the summer. I supply him—that's all."

"Sam," I said quietly, "did you ask Danny Marble to do you a favor?"

"Yes."

"What was it?"

"I—I gave him some heroin caps to plant in Caine's lab case. Something went wrong. I never found out what."

I glanced at Mark Storm, then said, "I'll tell you what I think went wrong, Sam. We almost caught Danny in Caine's cabin. He must have grabbed the case and ran to Rod's boat cave. He was going to escape in our boat, but we came down the hill too soon. Then he tossed the case into the water and hid."

"So, Danny Marble was our stowaway," Mark said, shaking his head.

"That's my guess," I continued. "He took the *Clementine* back to *Hell's Light*, tied her up and then swam to shore where he retrieved the metal case containing the heroin caps."

"Why did you want H planted in Caine's lab case?" Mark asked.

"To make him break when the police questioned him." I asked, "Who planted my gun in your bathroom window?"

"I—I don't know," Aces whispered. "Caine, I guess. I thought it was Swanson until we got together. Caine must have had an ally aboard the yacht."

"Sam, did you plant the arsenic in Decker's luggage?"

"I—don't know what you're talking about."

"Did you and Swanson send Decker a note asking him to meet Swanson yesterday at four-thirty at the chimes tower?"

"No. You can ask Decker if you don't believe me."

"Decker's dead, Sam."

Sam Aces tried to get up, choked several times and then fell back, gasping for air, blood streaming from his mouth again. "It—it—isn't—possible," he whispered.

"He was shot and hanged in the chimes tower."

"Where's Swanson?" Aces looked around weakly.

"Dead."

"Ann Claypool?"

"Dead."

"And Joe Meeler?"

"Stabbed."

"Lori? No, not Lori, too!"

"Sam, she's—"

Tears welled up in Sam Aces' eyes and ran down the sides of his face. He trembled violently. "I—I should have known," he said, trying to catch his breath. "I—should have known all the time, but I was too stupid to realize—"

The producer rolled over on his stomach, his hand

searching for the wound that was draining life out of him.

Mark got up, gestured to Chief Clements. "Have Caine brought in here immediately."

Clements went into the swimming-pool bar and brought Rod Caine back into the dining room. He was assisted by a deputy sheriff and the seaman, Carruthers.

Sam Aces was so near death that he couldn't move. His head lay twisted sideways on the floor and a stream of red ran across the planking. He stared at me as I knelt down and lifted his head into my lap. He seemed awesomely pathetic, like a dog crumpled on the highway, trying to make me understand what he felt, but unable to say it except with his eyes.

Mark bent over the dying producer. "Aces," he said softly, "will you point out the man who shot you in the back?"

For a long moment, Sam didn't move. His eyes remained riveted on mine as if he were trying to convey some vitally important message. Then, very slowly, he looked across the room.

Rod Caine took a step toward Aces, but was held back by the three men around him. "Tell them the truth, Sam," the writer pleaded. "Tell them I didn't do it! Tell them!"

Then, with the last ounce of strength in his body, Sam Aces lifted his arm and pointed across the room to where Rod Caine stood with his three guards.

"You were my friend," he whispered. "I—I should have known."

His arm dropped to the floor and he was dead.

I watched them carry Sam Aces' body down to a Coast Guard launch. The blood-stained boat Sam had used to travel from Avalon was also tied to the float.

Mark patted me on the shoulder as he prepared to board the launch with Rod Caine. "I'll see you on the mainland tomorrow," he said. "Come on, smile. You look like you've just lost your last friend."

I glanced at Rod. "Maybe I have. Mark, what did Aces' mean when he said, 'I should have known'? Known what?"

"That Caine was the murderer."

"But," I argued, "he'd already said he thought Rod had been the one who shot him through the window."

"That's right," Mark agreed. "But he was stunned when we told him about the others—especially his wife."

The other police officials and Coast Guard officers climbed aboard the launch. Dawn was beginning to light the morning sea and a breeze scattered salt spray across my cheeks.

"Look, Mark," I insisted, "Aces said, 'you were my friend.' Rod Caine wasn't his friend. He hadn't been his friend for a long time."

Mark pulled his hat firmly on his head. "Honey, you're just sniping in the dark. The thumbprints check. Aces pointed out the man he thought was the murderer. So there it is. Sure, a few loose ends here and there, but we'll leave those to the prosecution to nail down. See you tomorrow."

The Coast Guard launch slid away from the float, gained momentum and disintegrated in the shadow of the island. I walked back up the steps. Music still drifted from the swimming-pool bar where a few diehards were still drinking Sam Aces' whiskey. On deck, at the head of the stairs, was Carruthers. He smiled in a drunken, half-lidded manner, and moved toward the bow. I called to him.

"Yes, ma'am?" He tipped his hat and grinned broadly.

"Who has charge of all the small boats attached to *Hell's Light*?"

"I do, ma'am."

"Have you noticed any of them missing during the past few days?"

"No, ma'am."

"You're sure?"

Carruthers nodded. His grin seemed like an idiot's grin, fixed and cemented on his old face. "Is that all, ma'am?"

"No," I said. "How long have you worked on this yacht?"

"Long time. Years, ma'am. Why, I was just thinking, there ain't been so much excitement aboard *Hell's Light* since old man Aces fell off the bridge and broke his neck." He laughed raucously. It seemed like a poor thing to laugh about. His eyes rolled weirdly, seeming to whirl like pinwheels on the Fourth-of -July.

Suddenly, I stepped back, for the first time really listening to his voice, really hearing his laughter. They didn't seem to belong to the body.

He took a .38 revolver out of his pocket and leveled it at my heart. His hand trembled, but he still laughed. He seemed like some awful mirth machine at the Pike in Long Beach that got stuck and wouldn't stop until somebody smashed the mechanism.

"You're too smart, Honey," the laughing voice said over and over. "I always knew you were."

I shook my head, trying to shut out the sight, the sound, the laughter. "It—it couldn't be possible," I said.

"Ever hear of the wrong man," the voice laughed inside of Carruthers. "Well, I'm the wrong man and you're the wrong woman and this is the wrong world! Funny, Honey? You kill me! Really fracture me! Your expression."

"Then you're the one Aces really was pointing at."

"Yes, yes, yes," the laughing voice continued. "I thought he was dead. I was down taking a fix and when I came up they were having a little trouble with Caine so I volunteered my services. Then, when we got inside and I saw Sad Sam—" The laughter choked him, choked him double, choked him until he couldn't stand, choked him until he was lying face-down on the deck.

I kicked the revolver out of his hand, grasped him by the shoulders and rolled him over. He wasn't breathing. The idiot's smile was still cemented on his face. I reached inside my skirt pocket and produced a handkerchief. The cloth lifted a coat of makeup from the man's face. Underneath was a deep scratch on his right cheek. Underneath another layer was Herb Nelson.

EIGHTEEN

IT WAS DAYLIGHT BEFORE THE CORONER, MARK STORM and Chief Clements came out of the stateroom where the man who had died laughing lay, the idiot's smile still frozen on his lips.

Mark seemed brutally dazed as if he couldn't believe what his eyes had found under Carruthers' makeup. He stared at me for a long time and then shook his head.

"It's Herb Nelson, all right," Mark said. "Narcotics killed him. Stopped his heart like a clock." He tried to steady himself against the yacht's railing. "Honey, I just don't get it. Call me stupid. Call me anything. But—we were so certain that the corpse we found at Herb Nelson's place was—"

"Were we, Mark?" I felt sick at the pit of my stomach. "We weren't so much certain as we were stunned. We found a man Herb's size, weight and age, with his head and face bashed in, carrying Herb's wallet and wearing Herb's rings, and we were shocked to think it was a guy we'd idolized when we were kids. A guy who'd been a prince, a champion—" I covered my face with my hands. My God, I can still hear him laughing!"

Mark put his arm around my shoulders. "I'm sorry, Honey."

I wiped my eyes and glanced up at the big lieutenant. "You said a skid-row bum named Ed Walker was seen entering Herb's place about an hour before the murder. You said he'd vanished. How do we know he's not our mangled body in the morgue?"

"Yeah," Mark said. "I thought of that, too. From what I can remember, his build and characteristics were similar to Nelson's."

"You said he was a user. He could have been on the prowl for H, found Herb gone and torn the place apart looking for junk. Instead, he came across Herb's identification, his wallet and two of his rings. He even discovered an old coat of Herb's with initials embroidered on the pocket and he put it on. As he was leaving with the loot, Nelson appeared. Herb had probably been down the hall in the bathroom getting ready for bed and in a narcotic frenzy he grabbed his Oscar and started swinging. End of story."

"Oh, no," the lieutenant groaned. "Beginning of story."

"That's not the beginning, Mark. The beginning was—" I shrugged my shoulders. "Who knows—probably when Herb Nelson took his first pop. A big star trying out a new thrill and it sank him right to the bottom. And when he got to the very last rung, one guy tried to give him a hand—Sam Aces.

"Are you kidding?" Mark said, arching his thick brows. "Aces was the good samaritan who supplied Nelson with junk."

"Sure," I defended. "Sam even supplied his own wife, but he didn't want to. He admitted he was trapped—caught—probably even worse than one of his hypes."

"How did he help Nelson?"

'The only way he knew how. He tried to get him bit parts in TV shows. Then came that disastrous day when Swanson threw Herb off the set at Television Riviera. Herb's pride was deeply hurt. His drug-twisted mind craved revenge."

"So, what'd he do?"

"Rod told me the last he'd heard about Nelson was that he was working as a bartender's assistant at the Golden Slipper. I have a hunch Sam got him that job. I have another hunch that one night Swanson and Decker were sitting at that bar drinking heavily when Golden Boy ordered a screwdriver. The bartender mixed the drink and while it was waiting to be served, Herb slipped in some arsenic. I'm sure he didn't know that drink had been ordered for his friend, Sam Aces."

"Nelson poisoned Aces' drink intending it for Swanson?"

"That's how I figure it," I said. "He never admitted the truth to Sam because the mistake provided a brand new idea. Since Aces thought Swanson was out to get him, Herb decided to make it appear as if Golden Boy were threatening his life, too. Then he picked me out of the phone book, planted a few seeds of suspicion about Swanson and—you know the rest."

"But I don't know the rest," Mark said. "All I knew is Nelson must have killed Walker like you said. Sure it was a mistake on our part. The body was so badly battered we couldn't go on facial features. He had no living relatives, no birth certificate. He'd never driven a car, never registered his fingerprints with the Department of Motor Vehicles. He'd never been in the service or belonged to any special clubs or secret orders. I don't think he'd ever been fingerprinted in his life."

"Sure," I agreed, "we thought the corpse was Herb Nelson. But he didn't know we thought this until the next morning when he saw the headlines. So, after the murder, he went to his friend, Sam Aces, and pleaded for help and Sam hid Herb aboard *Hell's Light*.

"And then Seaman Carruthers was created when they realized a mistake had been made."

"Right. Being an old-time actor, Herb knew plenty about make-up and he developed a most convincing character. When the Catalina voyage began, he probably told Sam he'd keep a watchful eye on Swanson. From there he embarked on a warped, neurotic plan—to murder Sam Aces and have Swanson swing for the crime."

"But, Honey, that doesn't make sense. Sam was his friend."

"Mark, we're talking about a man who'd hit the very bottom—narcotics, murder. The needle was his only friend."

"All right, where'd he go from there?"

"He stole my gun out of Sam's stateroom and was planning to shoot Aces through the bathroom window, but somebody caught him off-guard."

"Who?"

"My guess is Ann Claypool. Herb was probably in the corridor checking the angle of the shot when she came along. He left the gun in the window and ran thinking she'd seen everything. But it's my hunch Ann wasn't in the least suspicious."

"You think he killed her because he was afraid she'd seen him with the gun?"

"Yes."

"But, Honey, how do you explain Caine's thumb-prints on her neck?"

"Sam Aces verified the fact that Ann Claypool told Rod to meet Swanson at his island cabin. I believe Rod's story. But it was probably Nelson we heard running outside on deck that night. Rod went to Ann's cabin. Meanwhile, Herb came back to my window. I caught him, so he pretended to be bringing me the breakaway knife he'd used earlier on Meeler."

"But, why the devil did he murder Joe Meeler?"

"Because Meeler must have been on deck when Danny Marble arrived with the *Clementine*. Nelson saw what Meeler saw—Danny tying up the cruiser and swimming away. He knew, also, that if the police tracked down Marble they'd find Aces. And he couldn't trust that the trail wouldn't lead to him. Somehow he got Meeler into the bar. He'd probably planned to show Joe that breakaway and then, when nobody was looking, give him the real thing he'd taken from the kitchen. But we made it easy for him."

"What do you mean?" Mark demanded.

"Remember, we arrived back here with Chief Clements and everyone came out on deck? That's when Herb plunged the real knife into Meeler. Then he wiped off his own prints, put Joe's hands on the weapon and escaped through a trapdoor behind the bar."

Mark wiped his big hands across his eyes. "Okay, I'll buy it. What about Claypool?"

"After he left my cabin he went back to Ann's door. He probably heard the windup of the fight between her and Rod and sensed the opportunity. He waited until she'd undressed and climbed into her bath. Then, he slipped in, struggled with her and finally pushed her under the water."

"That explains the coroner's verdict," Mark said. "Where do we go from there?"

"It's pretty obvious Nelson planted the arsenic in Decker's suitcase. Why he did it we'll probably never know. Evidently he was the one who picked up Decker's luggage that morning and carried it down to the float. When you discovered the poison he must have been afraid Max, under severe questioning, might recall who had the best opportunity to make the plant. So, after Max's disappearance, Herb found out where he was and sent that phony note about Swanson wanting to see him at the chimes tower at four."

"So, he maneuvered Swanson to the tower using the same excuse and left Aces alone at the house."

"Right. He also sent a note to Rod Caine claiming my life was in danger, hoping to lure him into Avalon.

"Smart," Mark said, rapping his knuckles on the rail. "But, look, this is four o'clock in the afternoon. How could he hope to pull this thing off in broad daylight?"

"The storm, Lieutenant, remember? It was raining so hard you could hardly see your hand in front of your face."

"Okay," Mark said. "He hung Decker, then took Swanson to the edge of the cliff and shot him. Then what?"

"He returned to the house where he'd left Aces and put a bullet in Sam's back."

"Then it's true," Mark murmured. "Aces never really knew who shot him."

I said, "He didn't know what had happened until we told him Decker and Swanson were dead and he saw Herb come into the room. Then he realized the truth, but it was too late."

"What do you figure he did after he left Aces in the house in Avalon?"

"He must have been badly in need of a fix. He went to the Villa looking for Danny Marble, saw Danny and his girlfriend coming out of my cabin and figured he'd find some caps inside.

"And while he was rummaging around," Mark continued, "you came back and he clipped you with the butt of his gun."

"That's the way I see it. From there he headed for *Hell's Light* where he guessed Sam had a big supply of heroin stashed away. He finally tried the storeroom, tore into several cases and found some caps."

"I'm with you now," Mark said. "Then Lori, also needing a pop, came wandering on the scene."

"Right. I don't know how he managed it, but he got her into a boat and over to Caine's island cabin where they apparently had a small blasting party which wound up with Lori dead."

Mark took out a pack of cigarettes and offered me one. "It all adds up, Honey," he said, staring blankly at the distant island.

"Does it, Mark? Does it add up?" I leaned over the railing and watched the sea push up against the polished white hull of the yacht. "Eight people are dead and for what?"

"Don't ask me," Mark said faintly. "I told you this was a rotten business. It squeezes your guts right down to nothing."

"Yeah," I said, taking a deep breath.

I walked toward the bow. The wind was cool. It whistled strangely in my ears. It sounded like laughter. Wild, unreasoning laughter that wouldn't stop.

I began to run.

Suddenly I remembered that laughter. It was the laughter of a little girl with blonde curls sitting in a dark motion-picture theater. The laughter of a little girl for a great comedian, for a man who'd always made people happy, a man everyone had loved. A man who'd been such a genuine humorist that at the peak of his career he'd predicted that, come what may, he'd have the last laugh.

I ran to the bow of the yacht and I threw my hands over my ears, but I could still hear it. Only now it wasn't my laughter any more, it was Herb Nelson's. His wild, maniacal laughter. And I suddenly knew his prediction had come true.

Herb Nelson had had the last laugh. Even if it killed him.